GW00391500

EXITS

and Other Stories

EXITS
and Other Stories

B. A. KENNEDY

QUARTET BOOKS

First published in 2008 by
Quartet Books Limited
A member of the Namara Group
27 Goodge Street, London W1T 2LD

ISBN   978 0 7043 7130 9

Typeset by Antony Gray
Printed and bound in Great Britain by
T J International Ltd, Padstow, Cornwall

Contents

For Gerda, Thomas, Jacob, and David

. . . all these, just for an instant, did indeed contrive to make him feel as if they were adrift at sea in a dazzling, windowless box, ignorant of direction or of any points of the globe, and with no way of telling.

WILLIAM STYRON, *The Long March*

Confined

My husband was building a prison. That was how the dream began: that he was building a prison of a new and ingenious design, unlike any built before.

He had designed the prison himself. So he believes, at any rate, though it wasn't actually made clear in the dream. But he remembers vividly a feeling of basking in approval as he worked, a barely containable delight, because everyone was so hugely and demonstratively pleased with what he was doing.

A deep square hole had been dug in the ground, ready to accommodate the new prison. The prison itself was to be a single cell, an approximately twelve-foot cube, intended to house only one inmate.

Everything inside the cube was white; floor, walls and ceiling were all painted white; and always there would be concealed electric lights burning, so that permanently this whiteness would never be less than absolutely dazzling.

There must be thousands of prison cells painted white. Probably millions, my husband said. But this one was to be painted in a different way, the effect of which would be to deprive the prisoner of all external reference points – to deprive him, eventually, of the recognition of any reality at all, whether exterior or interior.

The way it was painted – and my husband can't explain how this was achieved – was such that whoever was condemned to occupy the cell would lose all sense of space and distance. Nothing would be discernible, in this uniform never-ending whiteness. It would be impossible to say where the floor ended and the walls began, or where the walls ended and the ceiling began. Nor was there to be any furniture in the cell which might enable its occupant (who would be chained to the floor and immobilised) to gauge its dimensions.

As a further refinement the entire cell would be soundproofed, thereby adding to the prisoner's punishment that of perpetual silence.

I asked my husband, How would the prisoner be fed, in such a place, or attend to his other bodily needs? My husband shrugged. All he could say once again was that these questions hadn't arisen in the dream, so he couldn't answer them.

High above him, on all four sides of the hole, the crowds who had gathered cheered him as he worked. Once the crowds parted and the king appeared, wearing the robes and crown of a medieval king, sitting astride a horse and looking down with a smile that was like the bestowing of a truly marvellous gift. What more could one want, after all, than to please the king? What greater cause for happiness could there be?

Exactly how he proceeded with the work, or how long it

took, my husband was also unable to say. All he could recall were those feelings of pleasure and pride in his work, the cheers of the crowd, the approbation of the king – those, and the image of himself in the hole in the ground and the dazzling whiteness arising all round him. There was something unearthly in such happiness. It was greater than any happiness he had ever known or could have imagined – a state of blessedness, of ecstasy. *Sublime*, my husband said, shaking his head as if the memory were scarcely to be believed.

The final stage of the project was to fit the door to the cell in such a way that it would be invisible to the prisoner; would be no more than just part of that measureless and unchanging expanse in which he was to pass the rest of his life. For the first time, then, the unspeakable horror of such an existence dawned on my husband. To be condemned for ever to an absence of both sight and sound; to be denied all external stimuli and means of judgment; and to know, moreover, that there was no one in the world who knew or cared about one's predicament! It would lead to madness, surely, but how many months or even years of torment would have to be endured before madness mercifully descended? How would one recognise change in oneself, or the passing of time? How would one be sure that one existed, even, or that the life one had lived before was not a dream or hallucination of some kind, itself a symptom of madness? It was too horrible to contemplate.

His work finished, my husband again became aware of the crowds of people above him, who were shouting for him to make his way up to join them. (How could he see them, now that the prison was complete? Perhaps he couldn't, he said. But even so, he knew that they were there and calling for him to come up and enjoy the adulation that was his due.)

It was then, unable to find the door he had so cunningly built, unable to see anything but that near-blinding expanse of whiteness, like eternity itself stretching around him, that he realised the true purpose of his work. All along, it had been for no one but himself he'd been building the cell. No matter the cheers, no matter the king's approval, *he* was the prisoner. He thinks he screamed at that moment, but can't be sure. There seemed to be a scream sounding; it was louder and more terrified than anything he'd heard in his life, the scream of the betrayed and utterly despairing, but he has no memory of the sound. Perhaps it was a scream that sounded within himself but never left him, as if to compel for good and all the recognition that no one else in the world would hear from him again. He had no idea what crime he could have committed or, for that matter, under whose orders he had been working all that time towards his own punishment. But he must deserve to be punished, surely, or else why would it be happening?

It was early morning when my husband told me about the dream. Sitting at the kitchen table hunched over a mug of coffee, a cigarette burning between his fingers, he looked ashen and afraid. But he went off to work as always; and in the evening when I brought up the subject again, he merely smiled at the memory. It was a dream, wasn't it? And, since the analysis of dreams was something neither of us knew anything about, there was obviously nothing to be gained by discussing it.

Nightmares, he said, in an airy, dismissive tone. We all

have them; they're therapeutic, supposedly. And he picked up a magazine and turned its pages, bringing the conversation to an end.

Boy

November 20, 1963
Police have still not established the identity of the young
man whose mutilated body was found early yesterday morn-
ing behind a derelict gas station outside the town of —, AL, a
spokesman announced today. He described the case as one
of the worst within recent memory. Victim is understood to
have suffered multiple cigarette burns and stab wounds and
other injuries described as 'too disturbing to be released'.
Detective —, in charge of the investigation, told us: 'We are
all sickened by such a terrible crime. This boy could have
suffered for hours before he died.' Police, who have no
clear leads at the moment, are questioning townspeople
and searching the area.

Arriving this evening on the outskirts of a large town in
South Carolina, the boy sees a wide redbrick building with
the words SALVATION ARMY over the door. He crosses
the street, pushes the heavy door open and tells the man at
the desk how he's hitch-hiking to New Orleans to see his

elder brother who's stationed in the USAF there. His brother's being posted to Japan next week, he says, might not be back for months or even years. He's hitch-hiked all the way from Montreal, Canada, and now he's down to his last few dollars and can't afford even the cheapest hotel. The man listens to him seriously, then says okay he can stay overnight and leads him to a large room filled with trestle tables and benches where a number of men are sitting and eating. At the other end of the room there's a counter where someone gives him a bowl of tomato soup and a plate with a hunk of bread and a wedge of cheese on it. The boy carries his tray to an empty table and sits down and eats. There's two hundred US dollars in traveller's checks in his back pocket, but he's not about to tell them that! He'll need that money when he gets to New Orleans. He plans to stay there a while; at least, if he can, until the end of winter, when – though he isn't thinking that far ahead, because you never can tell – he'll hitch back to Montreal probably. He's pleased with himself for having tricked his way in here so easily. So sincere, he'd sounded! So earnest! And it wasn't something he'd thought about or planned, even. It just came to him out of nowhere, that story about an elder brother. That was why it was so convincing, he thinks, because it hadn't been rehearsed.

He's twenty-one, but could pass for eighteen or younger: a tall skinny loose-limbed boy in tan lightweight trousers, dark-blue shirt and red nylon windbreaker. Pale skin, pale blue eyes, blond hair falling unkempt over his ears and forehead, a scattering of freckles round the bridge of his nose. It's the face of plausibility – of innocence – which is useful sometimes, which has certainly been useful this evening, but which most of the time he sees as the most outrageous and undeserved trick life's played on him. Because he isn't that innocent, if people knew, there must be people twice or even three times his age haven't seen what he has. In the department store where he worked that summer, they said he was crazy thinking of hitch-hiking all the way from Canada to New Orleans, but that was because they were jealous of him, all of them stuck in their dreary lives because they'd never had the guts to break free. For them the department store was a career, a place to which they'd given their lives and therefore had to take seriously, while for him it was just somewhere to work a few months and get some money together. They didn't like him there, because of his habit of making fun of everything, treating it all as a joke. It was though he was turning them into a joke; he recognised that now and again, but still couldn't break the habit, couldn't hold back the mocking remarks which came from his mouth so suddenly they took even him by surprise. But whose fault was it anyway, that they were stuck there and forced to take it so seriously? Not his fault, that was for sure. It was no one's fault but their own, though there were times you'd think they blamed him for it, the way they acted towards him.

After he's eaten, the same man he spoke to before gives him a towel and a bar of strong-smelling soap and tells him he has to take a shower. It's policy, he says, everyone who stays there has to take one. The boy leaves the door of the cubicle open a few inches, so he can keep an eye on his clothes while he showers. The hot water feels good on his body; he lifts his face to it, letting it bounce off his forehead and run down his chest. And all for nothing, he's thinking, all free, gratis and for nothing! If they could see him now, those people who told him he was crazy! If they could see how far he's come in four days, how easy everything could be, if you just dared take your chances!

Showered and dressed again, his hair combed, he's shown into a room with two long rows of beds and wooden chairs in it. Nine or ten men are in there, the same ones who were eating supper before, talking quietly together at the far end of the room. Some of them nod or lift a hand to him, saying 'Hi' or 'Hallo, there' as he comes in and drops his pack on one of the beds. Then two of them come across and ask where's he from, where's he going, and he tells them the same story about his brother, almost believing it himself this time. They're genuine hobos, these two, characters straight out of a John Steinbeck novel, wearing faded jeans and dark jackets, their faces leathery and lined, eyes narrowed as if against sun or wind. One of them pulls a tattered map from his pocket, unfolds it carefully on the bed and shows him the route he'll need to take to get back on the road south tomorrow morning. The boy doesn't ask them about themselves, their own lives, but sits on the bed thinking how fantastic this is, being here with these real hobos, seeing a side of life most people never get to see. He feels an exciting kinship with all of them. They're all the same, he thinks, free spirits, scorning the rules the rest of the world obeys so blindly. His own family's part of that world, so he knows what he's talking about: his father a sombre round-shouldered man going into the same prison-cell of an office day after day for twenty-something years now, then coming home to bury himself in the newspaper or fall asleep in his chair in the middle of a TV show you'd have to be a moron to watch anyway. And it isn't like he gets paid much money at the end of it all. Money's just about the only topic of conversation in the family, his father always complaining in the same dull, hopeless voice, struggling to pay the bills that keep coming, his mother working out the price of everything to the nearest few cents, patching up her clothes so she doesn't have to buy new ones, patching up *his* clothes – biting off the thread, then holding up the shirt or whatever saying, 'There. *That*'ll hold for a while,' as if he's meant to fall over backwards in gratitude or something. And now they're both happy because his younger brother's got a job in one of the two banks in the town where they live. So proud, his mother sounded on the phone. 'We're celebrating,' she said, in an excited, almost girlish voice, 'your father's bought a bottle of wine to have with supper tonight.' *Really?* he wanted to say. *A whole bottle of wine?* But he kept his mouth shut and when he went back into the room where his friends were gathered he said in a comedian's deadpan voice, *Guess what. My brother's got a job in a bank* and all of them fell about laughing.

That was his little brother for you. The one who worked hard at school, who got up early to deliver the papers every morning and didn't even spend the money he'd earned but kept it in an old-fashioned tin money-box in his bedroom because he was 'saving up' – not saving up *for* anything, just saving because it was the sensible thing to do, because he might need the money one day and if he'd spent it it wouldn't be there; the one who not once had shown any desire to leave his hometown and see more of the world – who seemed barely to realise that their town was not, in fact, the world – and who you just knew would end up marrying some nice dull local girl and visiting the old folks with the grandchildren every Sunday. No wonder they adored him. What else was he, what else had he ever wanted to be, but a mirror image of themselves? Well, good for him. Good luck to all of them. He isn't asking their approval, doesn't need it, to live as he likes. Maybe they'll realise that one day, but he sure as hell isn't holding his breath.

He undresses down to his T-shirt and shorts and when the lights go out he reaches for the wad of traveller's checks in his pants pocket and slides it inside his pillow-case. Two more days maybe, till he reaches New Orleans. Anything might happen after that. This is what people don't see, or what they choose not to see, because seeing it would show them just how limited their lives really are. Anything can happen. Maybe he should send his family a postcard with that and nothing else written on it, let them figure it out for themselves, he thinks before falling asleep.

They're woken at six the next morning and he follows the others into the dining-room where they're given bowls of hot oatmeal and mugs of coffee. When he returns to the counter with his bowl and mug, the old man who takes them from him says, 'You get this too, kid,' and hands him a transparent polythene bag with two sandwiches and an apple in it. 'Gee, thanks, that's great!' the boy says, pushing the bag into his pack. He wonders if there'll be other Salvation Army hostels on his way to New Orleans. If there are, he could make the rest of the journey laying out money for nothing but cigarettes and wouldn't that be something to tell!

It's quiet and empty out on the street, the air cold on his face and hands as he slips on his pack. But it'll be hot later on, like it was yesterday: already the sky's high and pale blue over the rooftops, not a cloud to be seen. 'Lord, I'm ten thousand miles from my home,' he sings under his breath, but it feels even further than that – as though the boy who lived in that home is someone with whom he has only the remotest connection, someone he heard about once, or read about in a book. There's only this, right now: this strange town, the fresh cold air on his face, the silence in the street like a held breath, *anything can happen*. Nothing of his past has come with him into this bright brand-new world, it's like today's the first day of his life.

Someone taps him on the shoulder and, turning, he sees the man who showed him the map last night. 'Just along there to the lights, son,' he says, 'then turn left and keep going straight; two, three miles maybe . . . Good luck to ya,' he says, holding out his hand. They shake hands solemnly and the boy experiences an unaccountable sensation of loss as he watches the man walk away. They could have been friends, he thinks, they could have travelled together and watched out for each other, could have been like father and son: *Son*, the man had called him. There's a lump in his throat, the threat of tears suddenly, as if something's been taken from him he didn't know was there and can't put a name to even while knowing he's losing it. But then he's striding off in his own direction, crossing the street to get the sun, whistling. They'd envy him, if they could see him right now. The whole world would envy him, seeing him swinging so carelessly along the street, not even worried about how long he might wait for a ride because he has all the time in the world, doesn't need to know anything at all except that eventually, sooner or later, he'll get where he's going. And it's great to be walking, feeling the warm flow of blood through his veins, the pack so light on his back he hardly knows it's there. He wouldn't want a ride now, not even if someone were to stop and offer him one.

The street slopes downhill slightly and at the bottom the stores and banks and restaurants come to an end. Then he's walking past automobile showrooms and office buildings and motels and then they end, too, and he's in open country. After a mile or so the road bends quite sharply and he decides to stop for a while and smoke a cigarette. He slides off his pack and puts it down beside him and takes his cigarettes and matches from his windbreaker. He lights up and draws the smoke deep into his lungs, squinting up into the sun so it falls full on his face while he smokes. It's beautiful here, everything so sharp and bright in the early morning, the air clear as water and further away the haze lifting off the hills revealing a dark row of pines on the skyline. Food in his belly and money in his pocket and the sun shining: *This is it!* he's thinking, at the same time wondering what's waiting for him in New Orleans, eager to get there because whatever's waiting he knows it'll be good. It's there and waiting, only he doesn't know what it is yet: like someone saying they've bought a present for you, only it's a surprise present, you'll have to wait and see.

Maybe he'll find a job in one of those famous New Orleans nightclubs when he gets there. Washing dishes or something. Maybe there'll be a girl working there, a waitress, or even one of the dancers maybe – a cute little girl with a southern drawl, who'll fall in love with him –

Now there's a truck he didn't hear coming pulling up beside him and two men getting out. Both of them are big, dressed identically in broad-brimmed hats and black

leather jackets. Both are wearing sunglasses, both have
pistols on their hips, and one of them's carrying a rifle or
shotgun of some sort. Police, he realises, and wonders for
a moment, though in a distant unworried way, if there's
some local law against hitch-hiking and they're about to
arrest him. But no, it's okay, they're acting like they haven't
even noticed him, one of them going to the back of the
truck and out of view while the other, the one with the
rifle, goes out to the middle of the road and stands there
holding the rifle in the crook of his arm and looking one
way and then the other down the road. From behind the
other side of the truck, the first one reappears alongside a
group of maybe a dozen men, some black, some white, all
wearing blue denim workshirts and jeans and carrying
scythes. They move past him slowly, giving him not so
much as a glance; then they form a line at the edge of the
road and begin scything away at the tangled long grass and
weeds growing at the roadside. A prison gang, that's all it
can be, and the nearest one only a few feet away from him!

The two men in charge stand watching them for a while.
One of them's still out there in the road, but the other's
closer and he's the one who strolls over to the boy after a
few minutes, asks where he's going, and whistles softly
when the boy tells him how far he's come and where he's
headed. 'That's one hell of a long way . . . one *hell* of a long
way,' he says, and the boy says proudly yes it is, no one had
believed he'd really do it and now here he is in South
Carolina already. The man doesn't answer this, but takes a
pack of cigarettes from his top pocket, lights one and stands
there gazing off into the distance. The boy asks him if the
men they're guarding are dangerous criminals, or just people

who've been arrested for minor offences. Like this one nearest to them, he says, lowering his voice, what's he in for? 'Him? That feller right there? Killed someone in a bar one night,' the man says and the boy feels a shudder of excitement that's like an electric shock shooting through him. 'Christ,' he says, 'how long's he in for?' The man shrugs. 'Ten, twelve years . . . be out after seven or eight, prob'ly.' The boy's lost for words. A murderer working away almost right beside him, and with a scythe in his hand! Not that he's worried about that: nothing can happen, he's protected somehow, out of reach of all danger, just as he's out of reach of his father and all those other people who want to change him, to trap him. So there's no fear for himself, only an exhilaration made even sharper by the thought of how people will react when he tells them what happened to him. *I was just outside this town in South Carolina . . .* He can see them listening, all of them, eyes fixed on him alone, waiting to see what fantastic new story he's going to tell them.

'What about if they run? – if they make a break for it?' he asks. 'Do you shoot at them, if they run? Are there dogs you set on them?' He tries to sound knowledgeable asking these questions, as if they've sprung from some source more authentic than the few movies about prison life he's seen.

'No need to,' the man says. He pulls on his cigarette, flips the butt out into the road. 'All we gotta do is pick 'em up.'

The boy frowns. 'What d'you mean, pick them up? Pick them up where?'

'Home. Home's always where they head for. All we gotta do is go there and get 'em.'

'Huh,' the boy says. He's baffled by this information. More than baffled: he feels betrayed, wondering how can it be true, how can they all just go home when they could run away anywhere and maybe never be found? They're meant to be tough, these guys. You'd certainly expect them to be tough. And all they can do is run home like little kids and get picked up again. It doesn't make sense.

'That's all they want,' the man says, as if guessing what he's thinking, 'just get on home and see their wives for a while. Kids too, if they got 'em . . . Hope you make it okay,' he says with a wave of his hand and ambles out to where the other man's still standing and shakes another cigarette from his pack. The boy steps out into the road and looks back to see if there's a car coming. Crazy, going to all the trouble of breaking out just to be picked up after a few hours and taken back! They should go in the opposite direction from their homes, steal some clothes and money somewhere, then head for a big city where they could get lost in the crowd. That's what I'd do, he thinks angrily, I wouldn't ever let them catch me once I'd got out. He wonders if he should offer the man nearest him a cigarette, or give him the pack if he wants it, let him know they're both on the same side and he doesn't condemn the man the way everyone else does. But he doesn't move. It would be a pointless sort of gesture and besides, he thinks, the guards would probably take them off him anyway. He stands there waiting for a ride, still feeling that rage and bafflement at what he's learnt. If they really wanted to escape, they could just rise up and overpower these two guards. No one would know, even. They could be miles away before anyone would know. He could help them, if it came to it; could give them the money he's holding, tell lies about where they'd gone –

There's the sound of a car approaching and a moment later it comes swinging round the bend towards him: Ford T-Bird with shiny red and white paintwork, a man and woman sitting in front. He picks up his pack one-handed and holds out his other hand with his thumb raised. It seems like the car's going to roll on by, but then at the last moment it slows and stops and the woman leans out the window looking back at him: late twenties or early thirties, low-cut frilly white blouse, blue eyes and tight-curled black hair, shiny pink lipstick, smiling as she asks where he's headed. 'New Orleans,' he says, and she says, 'Well, we ain't going *that* far, darlin', but we can take you to Mobile or somewhere close to it. Can't we, Fred?' she says, and the man answers without bothering to turn and look at either of them: 'Sure thing, honey, whatever you say.'

'Great,' the boy says. He waits while the woman gets out, then throws in his pack and clambers on through and sits down. Fantastic! he's thinking, first car that comes along and it stops for me, first time that's ever happened! He notices as they ease forward and pick up speed that the man's quite a bit older than the woman, looks fifty or so, and he wonders what they're doing together, they sure don't look like father and daughter. This could be quite a ride, he thinks, leaning back and stretching his legs. He takes the cigarette the woman's turned to offer him, then leans forward to bring it to the lighter in her outstretched hand. His own hand rests on her wrist for a moment, steadying it, and as she snaps the lighter shut she gives him a smile so cool and slow, so perfect in its mimicry of the wet-lipped provocative smiles seen on the faces of movie actresses on movie posters, that his blood jumps. The man turns, or half-turns, from behind the wheel and asks if there's anyone waiting for him in New Orleans, if he has to be there at some particular time. Not at all, the boys says; though he'd like to be there before too long, he says, since it is his destination, after all, the place he's planned on going and where he wants to spend at least a few weeks if he can. But there's no one waiting for him, he says, no one there who knows him, even. 'That so?' the man says idly. He turns again briefly; the boy sees a thin, dark face, small lively brown eyes, thin black moustache. 'So you're a bit of a loner, then, a bit of a lone wolf?' he says. The boy grins: 'I guess I am,' he says. 'Well, that's kinda interesting,' the man says. He smiles suddenly, the very soul of conviviality, as though the two of them are the possessors of some hilarious secret. In the mirror above him his eyes gleam, his small white teeth gleam. 'We're kinda loners, too, me and Flo.' His hand reaches out and lights on the woman's shoulder. 'Ain't that right, Flo?' 'Sure is, honey,' she says. 'That's right,' the man says, 'that's exactly what we are, 'cept we've got each other, of course. Anyway,' he says, 'the thing is this: me and Flo, we're just sorta what you might call travellin', right now, just driving round the US of A and seeing where we get to. Know what I mean?' 'Sure do!' the boy says. He can hardly believe this conversation – can hardly believe he's met these two people, as adventurous as himself, real soul-mates, he thinks excitedly, and what a tragedy it would have been if another car had stopped for him first, or if he'd set out half an hour later this morning. Because they recognise it too, they're as pleased as he is that they've met.

They don't look down on him as someone younger and less experienced than them, unworthy of inclusion in their lives. No, they don't, they see him as a kindred spirit, the same as he sees them. It must be fate, he thinks, they must have been destined to meet.

'Okay,' the man says, after a while. He doesn't turn round this time, but keeps his eyes fixed on the road. 'Listen,' he says, in a light, almost indifferent tone, 'I've just had a kind of thought here, a kind of *notion* I'd like to put to you, and then you can take it whichever way you please, think about it if you want and give me your reply. Is that all right with you?'

'Go ahead,' the boy says airily. 'Shoot.'

'Seems to me like we're the same sort of people, you, me and Flo here. People who like to take chances, you might say. People who want to know what's round the next bend. Am I right about that?'

The boy laughs. 'Sure you are. Couldn't be righter!'

'Good,' the man says, 'I'm glad we're in agreement on that point.' He pauses, taking a cigarette from the pack in his top pocket and leaning over to the woman for a light. 'And, seeing as we *are* in agreement, maybe we should just all link up for a while. See a bit of the country together. Hit a few towns. Have a few good times. Drive on into Mobile, maybe. How does that grab you?'

The boy shifts his weight on the seat. 'Well . . . ' he says cautiously.

'Is it money?' the man says. 'Is that what's worrying you? That you won't be able to pay your way?'

'Well, yes, I – '

'Because if it is, then let me tell you right now, you don't

have to think about money. Not for a moment. Me and Flo
have got money, and plenty of it. Haven't we, Flo?'

'If you say so, hon.'

'I do say so.' He slows down, looking into the mirror to
catch the boy's eye. 'I'm making a guess here, so correct me
if I'm wrong. But seems to me you're the sort of person
who, if he did have money, would be more than happy to
share it with his friends. I bet you've even done it, before
now. Haven't you?'

'I guess I have, when I've got it.'

'That's what I thought. And maybe one day – you never
can tell – maybe one day you'll have money and we won't
and it'll be you taking care of us two. It ain't likely. But it's
possible. But right now it's us who's got the money and,
well, we've taken a kind of liking to you, I guess, we'd like it
if you rode along with us for a while.

'So how about it?' he says, over his shoulder. 'Are you up
for it? Are you up for a good time?'

'I guess so. Just as long as I get to – '

'Oh, you'll get to New Orleans, kid, if that's what's bothering you. We'll see to it personally you get there, you got my
word on that.'

'Well, okay, then,' the boy says. 'Why not?' he says,
laughing, the look on his face one of incredulous and un-
adulterated delight. A kind of fever has descended on him;
he wants to shout and sing and wave his arms in the air, tell
these people he loves them and thanks God they didn't
drive on by back there but decided for whatever reason to
stop. They won't regret it, he wants to tell them, he won't
disappoint them.

' . . . just keep on driving for a while,' the man's saying, 'stop at the next town and buy some liquor if we can find some; stop and eat lunch somewhere. Then we drive some more, and then we find a motel somewhere. And *that*, amigo, is where the *real* good time begins. Maybe you think you've known some real wild women before now. Well, let me tell you something – when Flo here cuts loose, you're not even going to *remember* any other women, not their names or where you knew them or anything else about them. You know what I mean?' He laughs breathily, shaking his head. 'Maybe you don't,' he says. 'Maybe you don't have the first idea, even. How old are you, kid? Nineteen? Twenty?'

The boy clears his throat. 'Twenty-one,' he says, trying to make it sound more than it is.

'Twenty-one. Well, take it from me, you're going to feel one hell of a lot more grown up tomorrow morning than you do today.' He chuckles, looking quickly across at the woman. 'You're going to see to that, Flo. Ain't you?' Flo doesn't look back at him but, turning, gives the boy the same slow, wicked smile as before. 'That's right, darlin',' she says, with a theatrical roll of her eyes, 'Flo is going to *complete* your schoolin' tonight.' She stretches out a braceleted arm from between the front seats and walks her fingers slowly up the boy's thigh. 'How you like that idea, little boy?' 'Fine,' the boy says, blushing, 'I like it fine.' Leaning back in the seat and stretching his arms across its width, he thinks how young and inexperienced everyone will seem when he gets back to Montreal, like people on a different planet, almost, because of all the things he'll know and they won't. This is the best trip in the world he's having and the best part hasn't even started yet! He thinks suddenly of his father and brother, sees them crossing the yard together to his father's car, stamping the snow from their boots before they get in, their breath steaming in the bright cold air. He sees his father pulling up opposite the bank to let out his brother, sees him leaning across to pull the door shut, watching proudly as his son crosses the street, thinking *Thank the Lord at least one of them wants to make something of himself*; not pausing even for a moment to wonder where his older son, his first son, is or what he's doing before he pulls out and drives on to the other end of town and his own work. They're just like that, his father and baby brother, just like peas in a pod, and the one thing spoiling the boy's happiness is the knowledge that neither of them can see him right now, they'll never understand how much he's getting from life, that they and all the sad bastards like them don't even know they're missing.

Reincarnation

After dinner this evening, when the six of them, Caroline and Paul, Sally and Graham, and their hosts Vera and Ken are sitting at the table over coffee and brandy, the question comes up, What if there *is* such a thing as reincarnation? Who, or what, would they like to come back as? What would they like to be, or to achieve, given a second chance?

Caroline's close friend Sally speaks first. She'd like to be a musician, she says. A pianist, if she could choose. All that wonderful music you could bring into people's lives, Bach and Chopin and all the others. You could live in that music – could make it your reason for living. She was given piano lessons as a child, she says, and one of the biggest regrets in her life – 'Not that there are *that* many,' she's quick to add – is that she didn't take them seriously or persist with them. Of course she wouldn't have become a professional pianist or anything; but at least she *would* have persisted, might have become good enough to play for her own enjoyment at least, and perhaps to teach her own two girls how to play. For almost as long as Caroline's known her, she's been aware of this wistful self-deprecating side to Sally's nature; it's as though she bears in herself permanently the consciousness of something lacking in her life, some precious element bafflingly absent or misplaced, for which she holds only herself to blame. Now as their eyes meet across the table, Caroline smiles at her and asks why should it be too late, she could start taking lessons again, surely? Sally smiles back gratefully at her. There wouldn't be any point, she says. 'Not at my age,' she says, and there's such sadness in her face for a moment that Caroline has to force herself not to look away.

Graham after a moment's thought says he'd like to come back as a newspaper proprietor. So that he could bring out a real newspaper, he says, a paper concerned with real fundamental issues, freedom and justice in the world, and not all that ego- and sales-driven stuff about scandals and private lives which even the so-called serious papers plaster all over their pages. And it wouldn't have any advertising in it, he'd be wealthy enough to be able to publish it at a loss. 'Though I guess if I was that wealthy,' he says with a grin, 'I might just forget about the paper and devote myself to a life of sin and self-indulgence.' Which causes a ripple of laughter at the table, *mightn't we all!*

Then it's Vera's turn and she says she doesn't know, she's never actually thought about reincarnation. But now that she's obliged to think about it, what else can she say except that she'd like to be the person who finds a once-and-for-all cure for cancer, who puts an end for ever to that terrible disease. And remembering that it's only a year since her mother died of cancer, the others gaze down at the table as though guiltily taking stock of themselves and murmur their agreement. Sally looks particularly shamed-faced, Caroline sees, probably thinking, And all I wanted was to play the piano, how self-centred can you get!

Vera's husband Ken says well yes, of course, that would obviously be the best thing in the world one could do, no one would dream of disputing it. But if he can be selfish for a moment, since this is after all only a game, personally he'd like to be reborn as a painter, if he could, a landscape artist. Not necessarily a great painter, or even a better-than-average one, but a painter who does the best he can and gains satisfaction from it. 'I'd certainly prefer being a moderately successful artist to being a successful film publicist,' he says, and the others nod approvingly, even if some of them are thinking, as Caroline is, that Ken's surely too enamoured of his life, too dazzled by the actors and actresses he's met, the travel, the premieres, all the ephemeral but irresistable glamour of his world, to want to trade it in for the role of an unrecognised and quite likely impoverished artist. It's a thought that amuses her at first, but then amusement changes to sadness as she realises that no one ever says they wouldn't mind coming back just as they are, or as anything at all, for that matter, just as long as they could come back, just as long as life doesn't end in dying and then nothing, all hope and curiosity gone . . .

'What about you, Caroline?' Ken asks, and she says she really can't think of anything in particular. All she knows, she says, blushing, is that she'd like to come back with the ability to find happiness in small, simple things and to make the people who matter to her happy. She says, 'Rather a small ambition, I'm afraid,' and Sally at once says no of course it isn't, it's probably the hardest thing of all when you come right down to it. 'I would call it a *noble* ambition,' Graham says, which despite the false and even patronising note in his voice makes Caroline suck in her lower lip and fiddle with her fringe, as she habitually does when embarrassed.

Now there's only her husband left. 'Down to you, Paul,' Graham says and all eyes are turned expectantly towards him as if, being the last to speak, he's probably going to be the most profound and revealing. He has that reputation, rather: the introspective one, the one who reads a lot, thinks a lot, who gives the impression sometimes that there's a bit of himself standing watching from the wings with a small knowing smile on his face. None of them, of course, knows him like Caroline does, and she feels a sudden apprehension as he picks up his brandy glass and tilts it slowly this way and that, all the time smiling to himself as if at some private joke he's just remembered. *Don't!* she's pleading with him silently. Telling herself there's nothing to worry about for heaven's sake, he isn't drunk, he isn't about to overstep any boundaries, but feeling nevertheless a dread so strong, so icy in her veins, that it's like a premonition. *Please, Paul. Don't.*

'A cot death,' her husband says, finally, 'I'd like to come back as a cot death, I believe.'

None of them says anything for several seconds. Vera makes a little sound somewhere between a gasp and a laugh. Then, 'A what?' Ken says. 'Are you serious?'

'Sure I am.' His face darkens, takes on that look of outrage and disbelief which might not be familiar to all of them at the table, but which to Caroline is frighteningly familiar. 'I mean who wants to go through all this shit *again*, for

Christ's sake? The same old shit! Isn't once enough? All this stuff about wanting to come back as a pianist, a landscape artist! Life would be just the same, if we all came back! Exactly the same! Don't you think we'd all be sitting round some dinner-table telling each other what we'd *really* like to be?' He shakes his head. 'Jesus,' he mutters.

This time it's Graham who breaks the silence. 'Seems like someone's had a bad week at the office,' he says, and everyone laughs too loudly and eagerly, with an almost palpable relief, at this explanation which surely none of them can believe. Vera gets up and begins collecting the used napkins from the table, and Ken pushes back his chair and reaches to the sideboard for the brandy. 'Who's for a top-up?' he asks, brandishing the bottle in an exaggeratedly festive gesture. Caroline doesn't look at her husband. She sits with bowed head, not looking at any of her friends at the table for fear of what she might see, what their faces might tell her.

Role

Almost four full days the sales conference had lasted. And it had been hard: immeasurably harder than the half-dozen or so he'd attended before the takeover earlier that year, in what he'd already begun thinking of (though aware that it was a notion owing far more to present anxiety than to past content) as 'the good old days'. Behind the analysis of sales by region, by product, by time of year; behind the compulsory self-appraisals and gruelling 'motivational sessions'; and especially behind the revised sales targets which were virtually unattainable, the work, he'd thought, of a lunatic or a sadist (and yet he had not really been affected by them at the time, had not even consciously responded to them with the old evasive formula *We'll worry about that when the time comes* but had read them with a kind of remote, hilarious disbelief) – behind all these things he'd recognised a message which, even though it had never been precisely expressed, could not have been clearer: perform or you're out! He'd been aware of it from the moment he'd arrived at the hotel, even before he'd taken his luggage from his car

and crossed the car-park: something chill and threatening
in the air, which had stayed with him as he'd unpacked
his clothes and sat on the bed re-reading the conference
schedule, and had only intensified throughout the following
days. In the past, when the company had still been run by
members of the family who had founded it, a generous
degree of democracy had prevailed, grievances had been
aired without the fear of recriminations, ideas for improving
the business had been listened to and even sometimes
acted upon. Now, and despite the fact that two of the old
directors had been retained on the board, there'd been the
chance to air no opinions at all. They'd been talked to,
talked *at*, as if they were born to be driven, as if beyond
their lives as salesmen they simply had no lives, or nothing
in their lives of such importance that they wouldn't hestitate
to sacrifice it if their work-lives demanded they should.
Even the few 'recreational periods,' so called, had been
arranged around the notion of competition, of winning: a
dauntingly hard quiz evening, which could only have been
designed to make them all feel lamentably ill-informed; a
snooker tournament (optional, mercifully); and, most out-
landish of all, a two-and-a-half mile early morning jog
around the perimeter of the hotel's grounds, for which
they'd been issued with shorts and singlets bearing the
new company logo. *Bloody Americans*, someone had said,
wheezing painfully alongside him, and what was truly under-
mining about the words was that they were the nearest
anyone on the sales force had come to protest during
the entire four days, at least that he'd heard. They were
American-owned now, after all, and for most of them
the chances if they were fired of finding work elsewhere

would be to put it mildly remote. The country was close to recession, was already *in* recession, some said, and although of course they were accused of trying to 'talk the country down,' the words had a demoralising ring of truth. It was not a time to be looking for work, it was a time to be grateful one *was* working, no matter under what conditions. *Gentlemen, I don't need to tell you, it's survival of the fittest time. No room for excess fat, no time for the weak and fainthearted* . . . It was insulting, above everything else. It was insulting because the man who'd spoken those words had already cut the workforce by close to twenty percent and had reduced the salaries of those who were left almost without exception. If he'd wished, he could have off-loaded the company tomorrow and shown a profit. It was insulting, too, because of what it told them about his view of their intelligence, their feelings, the simple fact of their existence as human beings and supposedly his fellows on the planet, even if his to command. And there was absolutely nothing any of them could do about it, which of course he knew, and knew that they knew he knew. Driving away in bright sunshine when the conference closed, he felt as though he'd woken from a dream so absolutely 'real' that reality itself had become the dream: his mind registered *clouds, houses, telegraph poles, trees*, all these things utterly familiar yet abruptly and mysteriously strange, so that there was a kind of wonder, a sense of achievement almost, in the mere fact of his being able to recognise and name them. He drove for a little more than an hour, then pulled in at a Little Chef where he sat by the window smoking a cigarette and slowly drinking his coffee. It's over, he thought, I should feel a bit better now. Yet looking round at the others in the

restaurant, families, couples, two solitary blank-faced figures
who were probably salesmen too, he experienced a sudden
hopeless and unfocusing yearning, a burning of tears behind his eyes. To be one of these other people, instead of
himself! To be going where they were going, no matter what
their destination! Why wasn't it possible? Why did he have
to be so inextricably himself, trapped in this particular life
until it ended? Where was the one who could lay a wise and
caring hand on his shoulder and help him find the way to
wherever it was he had once wished to go? It was not fair.
Life – or God, if there was one – had not been fair on him.
And then he pulled himself together somehow, ashamed,
reminding himself again that there were people in predi-
caments infinitely worse than his own, people who would
have counted themselves blessed if they could have changed
their place for his, and he paid his bill and sat in his car for
two or three minutes trying to calm himself before continuing his journey. Half an hour more on this road; then the
motorway, for a spell; and now (too soon, too soon! he
would have driven for ever if he could, secure and un-
reachable in his car, free, in his beautiful never-stopping
car!) – now at half-past twelve he's passed through the bleak
industrial outskirts of the city where he lives and is driving
through a leafy suburb towards his house. It's pleasant
enough, the street where he lives: tall three-storey houses
of weather- and time-darkened red brick, their facades
enlivened by balconies and whimsical little turrets, the
occasional piece of stained glass in their front doors or
upstairs windows. Business people like him live in them,
or people who work in the media or in some vague periphe-
ral way the arts, or who teach at one of the several colleges

in and around the city. Not so long ago – though it seems an age ago when he remembers it, seems like a previous life-time, almost – he and his wife had been on the most amicable terms with their neighbours. They'd helped in organising Guy Fawkes night for the children each November, there'd been dinner parties, Sunday lunch parties, people dropping in for drinks; there'd been the sense now and then of prob-lems shared, burdens lightened, a real feeling of community at such times. And then the children grew up, of course, their son is away at university now, just as many of the neighbours' children are, and some of their old friends have moved away altogether, their houses taken by people whose children are younger than their own and who have their own sets of friends. Things would have broken up anyway, he thinks, bringing the car to a stop alongside the pavement outside his house, then crossing the pavement to his front door and reaching in his pocket for his keys. Inside, the house smells like a house where a party's taken place and now every-one's gone and no one's bothered to clean up: cigarette-smoke, booze, a stale and unidentifiable odour of cooking. Looking into the living-room, where the curtains are still closed, he sees an empty wine-bottle on the coffee-table, cigarette-ash on the carpet; on the mantlepiece the flowers he gave his wife the day before he set out are now faded and shedding their petals. He draws the curtains back, then goes along the narrow hall to the back of the house and pushes open the door to the kitchen. His wife, who is sitting at the table in her dressing-gown, looks up at him without expression, or perhaps something faintly surprised, faintly amused in her face – something contemptuous, surely, in the very brevity of her glance? There's a glass of red wine on the table, with a half-empty bottle beside it. Her face is even puffier and more pale than he remembers, as she lifts it to him again and says in a voice that's a joke, the most cruel and deliberate parody of marital concern, *Well, well, well. So you're back then. How did it go?*

Walk

After lunch, when we've cleared the table and put the left-over food in the fridge, and I've sat down to look at the paper, my wife asks me if I fancy a walk. She says, 'It's ages since we went for a Sunday afternoon walk,' and I sense a note of reproach in her voice, as if she holds me to blame for this sad state of affairs or is annoyed with me for not having made the suggestion myself. But it's October, a cold, grey day; I'm not in the mood for a walk, or for any other activity. All I want is to stay indoors and read or watch TV, waiting for the long Sunday to end.

'Just to the park for a while. Couldn't we?' she says. 'For my sake?' At which I relent as I have to relent, push the newspaper aside, put out my cigarette, get up slowly from the kitchen table and, with a sigh just loud enough to be audible, go out into the hall for my overcoat and shoes. My wife gets up too, and calls upstairs to our son as she follows me: 'Dad and I are just going out for a walk, Jamie! We'll be back soon!' I imagine she enjoys calling this out, thinking it will prove to our son (and to herself too, she might have

hoped) that his parents are still a fine, happy couple, still,
after seventeen years of marriage, able to take pleasure in
such a simple thing as a Sunday afternoon stroll. But perhaps I'm reading too much into the situation, she may just
be giving our son necessary information for all I know.

Outside, she slips her arm into mine as we walk up the
quiet empty street. We cross the main road by a pedestrian
subway, enter the park through a pair of high wrought-iron
gates, then turn a corner on to a broad avenue between two
lines of elm trees. Just ahead of us, two young women are
striding along; they radiate an air of purpose and high
seriousness, talking rapidly and intensely about something,
one of them waving her arms. Further ahead, and about to
be overtaken by the women, a young couple dressed in
cheap baggy rain-trousers and anoraks are slowly pushing a
pram. We follow this couple off the avenue and along a
narrow path which twists through a tangle of trees and
bushes, then brings us to a wide expanse of grass which
slopes away to a lake. In the middle of this expanse are two
enormous cedar trees, their lowest branches just inches
from the ground. To the left, sixty or seventy yards away, is
the elegant Georgian house which was once the home of a
member of the nobility and now belongs to the National
Trust and is open to the public. My wife stops for a moment,
surveying the scene with that expression both pleased and
melancholy which people invariably wear when revisiting
old haunts. 'Isn't it nice?' she says, turning and kissing me
on the cheek. She gazes across the grass towards the cedar
trees and I'm sure she's remembering how we used to bring
Jamie here when he was small – how he loved to sit astride
those thick lower branches and, later on, to climb to the

higher ones, revelling in his mother's cries of Be careful! or
Come down, Jamie! which enabled him to believe he was
doing something far more dangerous than it actually was.
But what was so interesting, after all, about a small boy
climbing a tree? Small boys have always climbed trees, and
always will climb them. All I knew was that I was there
because I had to be there – because that was what you did
when you were a young couple with a child, so as to be able
to assure yourself at the end of the day that you'd used your
free time in some positive, beneficial way. And perhaps for
some people it was beneficial, but not for me. The thought
that I was doing only what thousands or even millions of
others were doing, because I had no choice but to do it,
made me feel that with marriage and fatherhood I'd come
to the end of my life – or, rather, that through no one's fault
but my own I'd reached a point where all that was left to me
was to fulfil a series of obligations which would last as long
as my life itself would. In those days, too, I could think only
of getting home from the park, of getting those tedious
outings over and done with. That was all I wanted: to get
home again, to sit in the warm and read or listen to music
without being disturbed. It seemed unfair that I had to pay
such a price for these modest pleasures, when the world
was full of people who demanded so much more . . .

Solo

He was twelve-and-a-half now, and at last one of the soloists in the choir. Until Easter that year he'd been wondering if he'd ever be asked to sing a solo; he was ready, he'd kept thinking, so why were all the solos given to the three boys above him in the choir, Eldridge, Woodgate and Bean, and once, humiliatingly, to Kilpatrick, who was one place below him? Then on the Sunday before Easter he'd sung the opening bars of the anthem, 'The Souls Of The Righteous Are In The Hands Of God'; and on Good Friday, in the choir's annual performance of Vittoria's St. Matthew Passion, he'd taken the part of Pontius Pilate's wife, singing, 'Have thou nothing to do with that just Man, for I have suffered many things this day in a dream, because of Him.' Both these solos were brief and uncomplicated, but the cathedral had been crowded as it always was during Easter Week and it pleased him afterwards to remember how he'd been only the slightest bit nervous before singing them; certainly he'd been a lot less nervous than he'd thought he would be, whenever he'd tried to imagine himself singing a solo. After Easter the sixteen choirboys had gone home for three weeks, but now they were back and settled as easily as if there'd been no holiday into the familiar routine of two practices every day, Evensong every day of the week but Thursday, and three services on Sundays. In the practice-room they sat at long tables forming three sides of a square, with the choirmaster, Dr Graves, behind the piano in the centre of the fourth side. Eldridge and Woodgate would be leaving at the end of this term, and Bean the following term, and then he'd be Head Chorister. He was one of those the smaller boys looked up to in awe, just as he himself had looked up to the older boys when he was small, seeing them not merely as boys who were older and bigger than him but as creatures of an altogether different species, invulnerable, godlike.

Now it was a Tuesday morning, the summer term less than a fortnight old, and they were practising the anthem they'd be singing at Evensong the next day. There was a treble solo in it, again not a long one, but still he was pleased when Dr Graves asked him to sing it, and he sang it confidently and easily in the practice-room. There was nothing to it, after all. He could sing better than any of them, he thought: better than Eldridge, whose voice was beginning to break; better than Woodgate and Bean; and certainly better than Kilpatrick who, despite having sung a solo before him, had not yet been asked to sing another. He had the best voice in the choir, no doubt at all in his mind; and none, it seemed, in that of Dr Graves who, at the end of practice, said how pleased he was with him, what a fine voice he'd developed. 'A fine, true voice,' he said, 'good as any I've heard.' Dr Graves was a tall heavily-built man, often amusingly absent-minded in his behaviour, who dressed in baggy grey or brown suits which always looked in need of a clean, and often wore an almost colourless pork-pie hat on the back of his head: a 'character,' really, revered by all for his devotion for more than twenty years to the musical life of the cathedral and the city. It was he, 'Billy Graves,' as everyone affectionately knew him, who'd made the choir into one of the best in the country; he, too, who for all his renown as organ tutor, University lecturer, conductor of the local Bach choir and composer of several pieces of sacred music, had been quoted as saying that of all his activities, none brought him near as much satisfaction as practising twice a day with 'his' boys. Never had he raised his voice in anger to any of them; there'd never been the need, because to offend or disappoint Billy Graves, who cared so much for them, would have been an act of betrayal. He loved them, valued them above everything else in his busy distinguished life. It was inconceivable that they could let him down.

Then the next morning something strange happened. In the middle of a history test, as he sat frowning and sucking his pen over a daunting series of questions on The Wars of the Roses, he experienced a sudden apprehension at the prospect of having to sing by himself. It had descended on him from nowhere, it seemed, and it was impossible to understand, since there was surely no need for it. But it wouldn't go away; it was as though there was another self inside him, someone who just wouldn't believe him when he insisted there was nothing to fear. A stranger, inside him and yet working against him, whose presence he could neither explain nor wish away.

After history there was break, followed by a maths lesson;

then after lunch there was cricket, which as a rule he threw himself into with a passion which simply allowed no room for anything else. Yet far from disappearing during this time, his apprehension actually increased. What if he opened his mouth to sing and no sound came out? What if he couldn't reach the high note at the end of the solo? *What if he were to faint?* – all these fears ridiculous, as he well knew, yet embedded so deeply now that it made no difference that he knew. By quarter-past four, when he was changing into his white shirt and Eton collar, with only five minutes to go before he'd be lining up with the others to walk across the green to the practice-room, he was wondering if he might die of terror. Or was it that he was hoping he'd die? Death would be better, wouldn't it, death was clearly all that could save him.

Then they were in the practice-room and he was sitting with his hand raised, saying, 'Please, sir . . . ?' and Dr Graves was giving him a friendly, questioning look. 'What is it?' Dr Graves asked and as if from a distance, or in a dream, he heard himself explaining how he had a bad sore throat suddenly; it had only just started, he said, and he didn't know if he could sing the solo this evening. Dr Graves looked at him for what seemed a long time. 'Very well,' he said finally, 'we'll have someone else sing it. Perhaps you can give it a try, Woodgate.' They sang the anthem in its entirety and he was careful not to sing too loudly. Two or three times, he touched his throat and coughed. He was ashamed of his deceitful behaviour, but not so ashamed that he regretted it. He'd escaped, hadn't he, he wasn't beside himself with fear any longer. It was an escape for which any price would have been worth paying.

And no one knew. Which was important, because if you did something wrong and no one else knew, it was almost as though you hadn't done it. This was something else he'd learnt in his young life, another lesson unconsciously absorbed.

When practice ended there were still ten minutes left until Evensong, more than enough time for the boys to file out of the practice-room and into the vestry to change into their cassocks and surplices. As they rose from their benches and moved towards the door Dr Graves called out his name, saying he'd like a word with him. 'The rest of you go on,' he said, and a few moments later there were only the two of them in the room and Dr Graves got up slowly from behind the piano and came and sat down beside him. 'What's all this about a sore throat, then?' he asked. 'Is it true? Have you got a sore throat?'

He was blushing; he could feel the blood rushing to his face. 'Yes,' he murmured, staring down at the scarred surface of the table, 'I have.'

'What's the matter?' Dr Graves asked. 'Can't you look at me when you speak to me? Can't you look me in the eye?' There was no note of accusation in Dr Graves' voice, if anything it was even quieter than usual, and somehow he managed to raise his head and say, 'It just came on all of a sudden, sir. I don't know where it came from.'

'I see,' said Dr Graves. He was silent a few moments, rubbing his chin. 'Well, I think perhaps we'd better take a little stroll together. I think we need a little talk, you and I.

'We'll just do a turn round the green,' he said, when they were outside, 'and then you can go on into the vestry and join the others.' They set off along the path, the green on one side of them and on the other a row of tall ivy-clad houses where senior members of the clergy lived. Dr Graves rested a hand on his shoulder. 'Now tell me again, would you? This sore throat of yours: is it real?'

'Yes, it is.' He coughed again, bringing his hand to his mouth. 'It is real,' he said.

'Well, I'm afraid I don't believe you,' Dr Graves said, his voice as quiet as ever. 'I wish I could say I did believe you. But I can't, I'm afraid.'

They stopped walking and stood on the path just inside the broad shadow of the cathedral. Dr Graves' hand lay on his shoulder like the weight of the world, the judgement of the world, and he saw that it would be pointless trying to evade that judgement by repeating his story, since Dr Graves clearly hadn't been fooled by it for a moment. It dawned on him, with the force of an absolutely unquestionable truth, that he was seeing himself now as he really was, that the lie he'd told had revealed the *whole definition* of his nature, and that even though he'd been able to hide this definition from himself, it could not be hidden from others. Fear, and shame of fear, and shame at what fear had brought him to: it was all there was of him.

He sniffed, making a wet, babyish sound, and fumbled in the pocket of his grey-flannel shorts for his handkerchief. Dr Graves said: 'I thought you'd been growing up a little, this last year or so. I thought you were beginning to mature at last, but it seems I was wrong.' *At last*: what did he mean by that? That the others in the choir had been growing up while he hadn't? That, without his knowing it, Dr Graves had been dismayed by his immaturity for years? He wiped his eyes and caught up with Dr Graves who had set off once more along the path and was turning now, leading the way back towards the cathedral.

'Well, we must see,' said Dr Graves. 'We must see what can be done. Perhaps I'll have a word with the Headmaster about it. In the meantime,' he continued, 'I really don't know what to say. I haven't the first idea what got into you, to tell the truth. And I don't suppose you have either, have you?'

He shook his head. No, no idea at all, he could not explain himself. He knew that nothing would be changed by an explanation of his behaviour, but he felt that at least something might have been salvaged, some tiny insufficient vestige of that 'maturity' Dr Graves had spoken of, in which he was so indefensibly lacking.

They were approaching the entrance to the cathedral: those two vast and famous oak doors, decorated with the intricately carved figures of saints and bishops and other revered, exemplary figures. 'I wonder,' asked Dr Graves, 'if you can guess just how many cathedral choirboys there are, in this country of ours?'

The question took him aback. It frightened him, because he felt Dr Graves expected him to know the answer. In a voice not much louder than a whisper, he said: 'I don't know, sir.'

'No, nor do I,' Dr Graves said. 'Nor do I. But at a guess I'd say – oh, probably somewhere between five and six hundred, I should think.' He was silent for a while, as if giving the figure time to sink in. Then: 'Five or six hundred,' he repeated, 'out of a total number of boys you'd have to measure in hundreds of thousands. Do you see what that means?' he asked. 'Do you see what I'm getting at, with those figures?'

This time Dr Graves answered the question himself. 'What it means, you see, is that you, and other boys like you, are in a *privileged position*. You have this gift, you see, this gift given only to a few. You receive a musical education given only to a few . . . but with it, as with all privileges, certain things are expected of you in return. Certain . . . *responsibilities* have to be shouldered, which other less privileged boys can avoid. It's the way of the world, you'll see that for yourself as you grow older. Think where we'd be, for example, if I were to announce just before Evensong that I couldn't play the organ because I was afraid. Think of all those boys before you – and the ones still to come, for that matter – who'd be proud to sing a solo and would sing it as well as they could, no matter how nervous they might be.

'If it had been your first solo,' he went on, 'I could have understood. I've seen that happen, very occasionally. But you've already sung two solos, and sung them well. I can't think what's got into you.'

He fell silent again. Then he said: 'Well, we shall just have to wait and see, I suppose. We shall just have to keep an eye on you.

'We have to make the effort, sometimes. That's what it boils down to, in the end. We have to be strong enough to face up to these challenges, when they arise. It's what makes men of us.

'Now go along to the vestry and get changed,' he said, 'and I hope you'll try to remember this conversation, if only for your own sake.'

At last now he raised his tear-stained face to that of Dr Graves – who was looking down on him with such heaviness, such infinite sadness in his eyes! – and managed to get out the words 'Thank you, sir.' Then he entered the cathedral, making his way past stained-glass windows which gleamed in the late afternoon sun, throwing pools of colour on to the flagstones, past the tombs and effigies of the great and the good, and up the three steps into the vestry. None of the other boys spoke to him as he hung up his jacket and took his cassock and surplice from his locker. But they were looking at him, he could tell, even though he was not looking back at any of them. It was as though the choir had been divided abruptly into two distinct factions: the fifteen others, who had earned the right to be here, and could live up to it, and he, who had not. They would have seen he'd been crying, and he sensed that they were pitying him, and that they felt in pitying him a gratifying superiority. He sensed that they were terribly eager to know exactly what had taken place outside the cathedral, yet felt unable to ask. And, if they had asked, what could he have told them? That he'd become afraid, suddenly? That he didn't know why? His face burned, as he pulled his surplice over his head. Tears were threatening again and he clamped his lips tight. Half an hour later during Evensong the choir sang the words, 'I will arise and go to my Father, and will say unto Him, Father I have sinned against heaven and before Thee, and am no more worthy to be called Thy son.' He was to think of this repeatedly throughout his life as the consequence of some divine pre-arrangement: God had known all along who he was and, because it was clearly for 'his own good,' had devised this means of showing him to himself. He believed this implicitly in his later years, even though as a rule he chose to define himself as an agnostic tending towards atheism.

He couldn't explain why he'd been so afraid: that was the truth of it. But to insist that he didn't know where the fear had come from – to say *It wasn't me! It came out of nowhere!* clinging to the deceit that he was not to be blamed for what he'd done – would be so cowardly a lie that it would only compound his disgrace. He understood that. He understood that it was no use complaining that it was not fair he should have to pay such a price, when he'd been at the mercy of forces stronger and more baffling than anyone could resist: others, as Dr Graves had made only too clear to him, would have resisted. After the service, when they'd changed out of their choir clothes and formed up in a crocodile to walk back to school, and none of the others had said so much as a word to him, he thought how easily he could have sung that solo. It was nothing really, nothing at all, and if he hadn't given in to his fears he would have sung it and would be feeling every bit as pleased with himself now as he had after the two solos he'd sung before. But that was the same, he realised, as wishing he could be someone other than the boy he was, so instead as he walked he tried to look to the time when this evening would be part of his buried history, forgotten by both him and everyone else, so it would be as though it had never occurred.

Treasure

As a small boy he played repeatedly that game popular with children then, of seeing how far he could walk along the pavement without treading on any of the cracks between the paving-stones. It was harder than it sounded, though he couldn't believe anyone else found it as hard. His attention was always being caught by something, a car or bus passing, a dog coming towards him, his mother suddenly speaking. Even if there weren't any external distractions, in almost no time his mind would drift away from the pavement and into some dreamy oblivious world of his own. When he looked down and saw that his shoe had landed on a crack, he felt not just disappointed but acutely anxious, convinced that with his failure to concentrate he'd brought down some unspecifiable but terrible punishment on himself. He'd turn pale, hunch his shoulders, look round with a fearful expression, unable to tell how or from where disaster might strike. Not once did it occur to him that this was only a game, that there were no consequences attendant upon failure, and that if he didn't want to play it there was no one to tell him he must.

* * *

After lunch every day Mummy and Daddy went upstairs for a rest, leaving him to read or play quietly by himself during the long afternoons. Often he lay on the carpet playing Ludo or Snakes and Ladders or Beggar My Neighbour, taking the part of both himself and his opponent – 'the other,' to whom losing was as demoralising as if he were an actual other. The house they lived in looked out across the road to the floral gardens, bright in summer with flowers whose names he didn't know, then past the gardens to the promenade and the bandstand from which, on summer Sunday evenings, the faint sound of brass band music would enter his bedroom. Then there were the railings and the steps down to the shingle beach, invisible from the window where he stood, and beyond them the sea (on which sometimes, far off, he would see a ship slowly passing) and the usually rather misty horizon. In August troupes of holiday-makers passed by the window: families with small children, who carried buckets and spades, towels, picnic hampers, beachballs whose festive colours filled him with a longing he was too young to recognise as longing; often, both grown-ups and children were eating ice-cream. There was something mysterious in the sight of all this activity; he seemed to be looking at things which had names but no meaning, as though he had learnt their names by rote. Occasionally someone would glance towards the house and see him; occasionally whoever had seen him would give him a wave and a smile and he'd immediately blush and move quickly out of sight, as painfully self-conscious as if the person smiling had seen some kind of strangeness or deformity in him and was laughing at him rather than smiling. He had never been on holiday; Daddy was much older than Mummy and had a 'bad heart;' that was why Daddy didn't like to go very far, or exert himself too much, that was why Daddy had had to sell the company he owned, and why it was so important not to make a noise and disturb him while he was taking his afternoon nap. Poor Daddy, who had had so much energy when he was young, had started his own engineering company and built it up – he was still a 'major shareholder,' Mummy said – and then out of nowhere this horrible illness, this 'heart trouble,' from which he had still not fully recovered. They'd never really expected to have children, and when they were told one was coming anyway they'd hoped for a girl; girls were so much quieter and less troublesome, as a rule. Actually, Mummy said, when they told her the new arrival was a boy, 'I swore and cursed like a trooper – words I'd never uttered in my life before, and never have since.' But she'd got over it, of course; both of them had. A baby was a miracle, after all, a baby was a gift from God, and once that first shock had worn off she and Daddy were as delighted as any new parents. It was just that Daddy wasn't as young or as well as he'd like to have been, to have a boy in the house. Mummy said she hoped he understood that and would be a good boy for Daddy's sake. And he was a good boy. Not once during those solitary afternoons did he make any noise in the house or do anything else to disturb Mummy and Daddy while they were sleeping. Even when he needed urgently to go to the lavatory, he would force himself to wait until Mummy and Daddy were awake and downstairs again, for fear he might wake them pulling the chain. The afternoons passed slowly, soundlessly but for the ticking of the grandfather-clock in the hall, so that life seemed to have become the same afternoon going on for ever.

*   *   *

'Where's my little boy!' Mummy said when she at last came downstairs. She was wearing her dressing-gown, a billowing, dark-blue silk robe, on its back an exotic bird coloured green, yellow and red, a creature which both fascinated and frightened him. He was an absolute treasure, Mummy said, there couldn't be any little boy in the world more considerate. She kissed him, holding his face between her hands: 'The best little boy in the world, no wonder Mummy loves him so.' She drew him against her and he felt the soft warmth of her body, smelled the clean smell of her dressing-gown mingled with that of her talcum-powder and the giddying perfume she wore. (It was called *Chanel*, he'd seen the bottle on her dressing-table.) He felt safe in these moments, enveloped by that pliant fragrant warmth. It was where he belonged, his shelter from all fears. He wanted to stay there for ever and, when she was hugging him like that, was able to believe that he could.

In the kitchen, after she'd put on the kettle for tea, Mummy gave him a glass of orangeade and let him stand on a chair to lift down the biscuit-tin from the shelf and take two chocolate biscuits from it. He ate them gravely, careful afterwards to lick all the crumbs and melting chocolate from his fingers so there wouldn't be chocolate all over the tin when he put it back. Mummy poured the hot water into the pot, called up from the foot of the stairs, 'It's on the table, Daddy!' and a little later Daddy came down. Daddy walked slowly about the house; in the kitchen his slippers made a scratchy-shuffling sound on the tiled floor. He sipped his tea, pausing between sips to glance out of the window or to take off his glasses and gaze around the kitchen with a puzzled look in his watery blue eyes, as though he'd woken to a place he didn't know. Sometimes after tea he went out and looked around the garden, bending to examine the flowers, now and then lifting one and sniffing at it, or bending to pick up a stone from one of the flowerbeds and then tossing it towards the rockery. Daddy couldn't do the heavy work any more, they had to pay someone to do it; but still sometimes he went back and forth in the garden, always with the same slow, measured steps, filling the watering-can from the outside tap and watering the flowers and the few redcurrant and raspberry bushes in front of the back fence. During this time, when Daddy was outside and Mummy was in the kitchen washing up the tea things and putting them away, he could perhaps have played more boisterously if he'd wanted. But there was nothing to play, or anyway nothing he could think of. Soon, in any case, Mummy would go upstairs to get dressed and when she came down again it would be time to start getting supper ready. This was another of the nice times, because he and Mummy were alone together again (if not in the garden, Daddy would be sitting in the living-room reading or listening to the wireless) and there were all sorts of little ways in which he could help Mummy with supper. He could go into the dining-room and take the plates and the cutlery and the serviettes and the glasses from the sideboard, he could throw the potato peelings into the bin, or open the cupboard under the draining-board and take out the pots and pans Mummy needed. There were all sorts of things he could do, and Mummy never failed to say how lucky she was, to have such a devoted little helper.

*   *   *

The Wicked Witch lived in the picture on the landing, just outside the door to Mummy and Daddy's bedroom. Really there wasn't any witch in the picture, just a stream with a tree leaning over it, painted in what Mummy said was 'the Japanese style'. But it was Mummy, too, who'd shown him how if you looked carefully at the tree, you'd see it was exactly like a witch. *There's her eye, there's her long nose and long curvy chin . . . See, darling? See the Wicked Witch?* Mummy poked him in the ribs; she made a cackling sound, at which he jerked his head back in panic. 'Don't you worry, sweetums,' she said, ruffling his hair, 'it's only naughty little boys the witch doesn't like.' He didn't want to ask, but the question was out before he could help it: 'What does she do with them, Mummy? With the naughty little boys? What does the Wicked Witch do with them?' 'Ooh, I don't know, darling. Carries them off on her broomstick, I shouldn't wonder. Cooks them in a pot and eats them for dinner, there's no telling what a witch might do.' He wasn't so afraid in the daytime, though sometimes when he was upstairs he had to force himself to stop and look at the picture, telling himself of course it wasn't a witch, it was just a tree, anyone could see that – except that it was impossible now *not* to see the witch, so evil-looking with that gleaming malevolent eye and horrid curved chin! But still he managed to turn away and hurry downstairs into the living-room or the kitchen or wherever else Mummy might be. Then he forgot about the witch, but only until bedtime. In the darkness there was no escape. Once he told Mummy about the Wicked Witch and asked her if she could leave the light on after she'd kissed him goodnight, but Mummy said no she couldn't. It would be bad for him, she said; he'd get used to

having a light burning and might never be able to sleep in
the dark again for the rest of his life. And anyway, there was
no one there, no Wicked Witch, nothing at all in the dark to
be afraid of. So he lay in bed as he always had, just a thin
shaft of light entering the room where Mummy had left his
door open an inch or two. No escape, nowhere to hide. He
turned on his side and immediately the Wicked Witch was
crouched behind him by the headboard, grinning her terrible
grin, preparing to carry him off. Terrified, he forced himself
to turn to catch sight of her – if he saw her she would
disappear, he believed – but no matter how swiftly he
turned the Wicked Witch moved more swiftly still, leaping
noiselessly over the bed so as to be behind him again. It was
no use, trying to see her; she was too fast, too evil; her
powers were too great. She wanted to frighten him first,
and then she'd throw him across her broomstick and fly
away with him out of the window and far off into the dark.
If Mummy would let him have the light on! If he could call
to Mummy and let her see how afraid he was! But Mummy
and Daddy were downstairs having their 'quiet time' together (that was how Mummy spoke of their time after he'd
gone to bed); if he called she'd be angry with him and who
knew then what might happen? She might close the door
altogether, so the bedroom would be darker still. He wouldn't
be her little treasure any more, if he spoilt her quiet time.

He slept, eventually. But suffered nightmares sometimes,
of which he had only the most fragmentary memories when
he woke: luminous flapping birds with fierce beaks and
talons sharp as the sharpest knives swooping down on him
in the dark; sometimes the glittering multicoloured bird on
Mummy's dressing-gown. But then it was daylight again

and he didn't think about his dreams or the Wicked Witch. He forgot that another night lay ahead. There was the day first, and Mummy would be there. Mummy would shield him from the Wicked Witch, and from anything else that might harm him. He'd look at the picture again and this time there wouldn't be any witch: only the tree, which was nothing else but a tree, and the stream running below it, and the spiky tufts of grass on the banks.

*   *   *

Daddy was pleased with him, wasn't he, for being so good? Daddy must be pleased with him. Yet he always felt uncomfortable and even ashamed in Daddy's presence, as though already it had been revealed to him that he could never please Daddy, nor even find in himself any meaningful way to try. 'Daddy loves you, darling,' Mummy had said – 'Just like I do!' But he'd never heard Daddy say it, or seen any sign that he was pleased.

Daddy played little games sometimes. For example, coming into the room and looking at him with eyes widened as though in amazement behind his glasses, throwing up his arms, asking, 'Who's *this* little chap, then? Who's this *serious . . . solemn . . .* little chap? What's he doing here?' And once, turning to Mummy who'd come in behind him, and still in that same astonished tone: 'Did *you* ask him in? I certainly didn't.' Mummy must have seen something in his face then, because she hugged him quickly and said through her laughter, 'Don't look so worried, darling! Daddy's teasing – you know he's just teasing!' He didn't feel any better for being hugged. He was supposed to have responded to Daddy in some way, just laughed like Mummy perhaps, but he was too confused and too ashamed of his confusion to laugh. He was here in this house with them, but he wasn't really meant to be here; it was a mistake of some sort; was that what Daddy was saying? But if not here, then where? In some other house, with a different Mummy and Daddy? Was that where he belonged? And those words Daddy had used: Serious. Solemn. They weren't good things to be – couldn't be, or Daddy wouldn't have spoken them in that tone. It was – feeble, somehow, to be serious and solemn. It was not what he ought to be, not what Daddy wanted.

Other times Daddy would ask him in a gruff, hearty voice, not like his usual voice at all, 'Well now, young feller-me-lad, and what have you been up to today? Mischief, I'll be bound.' He'd giggle then, recognising that Daddy was only playing. But still at the same time he'd blush and hang his head, or look awkwardly away. There was something more required of him, again some particular response Daddy was waiting for, only he couldn't give it because he didn't know what it was.

On Saturday mornings, as soon as Daddy had eaten his toast and drunk his tea, and swallowed the several pills he had to take every day, he went into the conservatory and sat down at his desk with his funny pink-coloured newspaper and an exercise-book and a ruler and pencil. This was a time when again it was necessary to be quiet, because it was important work Daddy was doing, 'checking his stocks and shares'. When he asked, What are stocks and shares, Mummy? Mummy said he was too young to understand just now, she'd explain it to him when he was older. Or perhaps Daddy would, when the time was right. All he needed to know for the time being was that it was the stocks and shares Daddy bought which brought in a good deal of their income, so of course Daddy had to keep a watchful eye on them, to make sure they were going up and not down. 'Daddy knows his duties to us, darling. Someone else might just forget about their investments and hope for the best. That's not Daddy's way, though. Daddy wants us to be well provided for, wants us not to have to worry about things. That's why he stays in there so long – to be sure it's a good idea if he's thinking of selling some of the shares and buying others.' So far, Mummy said, Daddy had done very well indeed, better than he'd hoped for, even. There'd been shares that had fallen sometimes – there were bound to be – but the 'whole portfolio' had risen regularly each year, often by as much as ten or eleven percent. 'Daddy's very clever, darling. And very kind-hearted, to take care of us so well. You'll see that one day.'

After he'd helped Mummy clear the breakfast things away and take the cloth off the table, he sat down in the living-room and pretended to read 'The Squirrel, The Hare And The Little Grey Rabbit'. (Poor Little Grey Rabbit, who was so kind to Squirrel and Hare, was treated so cruelly by them, yet still to save them consented to have her beautiful fluffy white tail cut off! It had been his very first book and was still the one he returned to most often.) From the arm-chair where he was sitting he could see Daddy through the wide glass doors which opened on to the conservatory. Daddy sat at his desk peering at the newspaper, peering at his open exercise-book lying next to it, then picking up his pencil and ruler and ruling a line in the book. He frowned sometimes, or raised his eyebrows, or shook his head. Then he closed the book and pushed it to one side and spread out the newspaper on the desk. His face still kept changing as he turned the pages; occasionally he picked up his pencil again and marked something on the page he was reading. Watching, he felt closer to Daddy than at any time; felt that by being as close to him as he was, and by keeping quiet, he was helping Daddy with his important work – though, at the same time, he was afraid tha*t* Daddy would look up and see him watching and would be disturbed in his work and angry, which was why he dared sneak only an occasional glance at Daddy. Eventually Daddy folded the newspaper and gathered up the rest of his things and came back blinking into the living-room, wearing the same look he wore when he came downstairs at tea-time after his rest. Daddy went through the room and into the hall without saying anything – without even noticing there was anyone there, it seemed – and a few moments later there were the sounds of his voice and Mummy's from somewhere else in the house. He couldn't make out what they were saying and their voices gave him a hollow frightened feeling. Quite some time went by before he was able to calm down and lose himself in his book.

*   *   *

At school – St. Dunstan's Preparatory School for Boys, the most expensive school in the area, Mummy said, and widely regarded as the best – he worked hard at his lessons, not knowing how to do otherwise and convinced, even though he regularly scored higher marks than anyone else in his class, and was frequently praised by the teachers, that his best wasn't good enough. They were praising him because they were sorry for him, it wasn't like real praise.

When not ignored, he was picked on and ridiculed by the other boys. Not as much as Catesby, who lisped, or Jupp, who had a club foot which he was often compelled to display, but often enough that the fear of being picked on was constant. In the playground someone would barge into him, sending him stumbling backwards against the red-brick wall; then another boy would barge into him, and another, until either they lost interest or the bell sounded, calling them back to their classrooms. After school, he sat in the dining-room doing his homework, rarely raising his eyes from his books, fearful of having to cross something out or of spilling ink on the page, praying he'd be left alone the next day. If he'd been able to join in their games, it wouldn't have mattered to them that he worked so hard and did so well, but he didn't know how to join in. Playing and fighting came easily to them, activities they were born to and pursued with a ferocious and uninhibited joy, but for him the effort of will it would have cost to try to join in was simply beyond him. And would be futile anyway, because if you had to try then you couldn't help but fail. His fate was simply to endure whatever discomforts they inflicted on him, to be grateful for the days when they seemed not to notice him and, if only for a while, he could forget everything else and immerse himself in his work.

*   *   *

He was eighteen when his father died; had left school with seven 'O' levels and three 'A' levels and been offered a place at one of the more prestigious universities. His mother said she was glad Daddy had known that before he'd died; he'd been so proud of his son, even though he might not have

shown it, she said. (In fact, his father had said in an embarrassed voice, without really looking at him, 'Well done,
old boy. Congratulations' and had then turned and picked
up the clock from the mantlepiece to wind it. He'd taken no
pleasure from the words, had not even believed them really.)

And thank heavens Daddy hadn't suffered any pain, his
mother said (she had never called him anything but Daddy,
even to his face). Daddy had been sitting out on the patio
when it happened, just sitting in the sun reading the paper,
as he so much enjoyed doing when the weather allowed.
There'd been nothing in his manner that morning to suggest
there was anything wrong. But at eleven, when she opened
the kitchen window to ask if he'd like a cup of tea brought
out to him, she saw the paper lying on the brickwork, fallen
from Daddy's grasp, its pages fluttering weakly, and she
saw that Daddy's head had fallen forward and that he was not
moving. 'He died peacefully, darling, sitting in the garden
he loved. We have to be thankful for that.' At the funeral he
stood with his mother feeling false and insufficient in his
suit and collar and tie; his arm linked with hers, he watched
his father's coffin being lowered inch by inch on ropes into
the grave. *Man that is born of woman,* the vicar read out;
and presently, following his mother, he stepped forward to
toss a single red rose on to the coffin. It had been raining
earlier, and although the rain had stopped some time ago
and the sun was shining, it was still damp underfoot. He
was convinced he was going to slip on the grass and topple
forward and fall into the grave himself. Numb, his legs
moved more like his father's than his own. He was afraid
he was going to faint.

'Daddy's been very good to us, dear. Better than I knew,

even.' His mother was sitting at the desk in the conservatory – Daddy's Desk, which no one but he had ever
opened and which had always been kept locked when he
wasn't using it. He knew it was necessary to go through his
father's papers, but it didn't seem right. He felt that his
father was watching from somewhere, angry at this in-
trusion into a place which had been his alone and should
have remained his. He felt that it was him, not his mother,
whom his father would be blaming. There was that dread in
the pit of his stomach, as though he'd been caught in an act
for which there could be no defence, no excuses. It might
have been God whose anger he'd aroused.

There were papers everywhere: on the desk, on the low
glass-top table next to the desk, on the flagstone floor. Daddy
was a good man, his mother said. If anyone had doubted his
goodness, though heaven knows there was no reason why
anyone should have, the provision he'd made for his wife
and son would have dispelled their doubts for ever. Aside
from all those stocks and shares he'd looked after so well,
and the large number of shares in the company he'd had to
sell, Daddy had taken out two life insurance policies, both
before he'd fallen ill, fortunately; they'd bring in either a
substantial lump sum or a useful income, his mother said,
or a combination of the two if they chose. And there was
more: money invested overseas, money in a 'high-interest
deposit account' which he had never so much as mentioned.
How much it all added up to was impossible to say, but it
would be enough or even more than enough for them to live
on.

'A good man . . . ' his mother repeated, this time in a
choked, trembling voice, and when she rose from the desk

and her face caught the light for a moment he saw that there were tears in her eyes. He wanted desperately to do something about those tears, to say something that would comfort his mother, but he was panicked by the sight of them and the words wouldn't come. After a time he moved stiffly to her side, laying his hand on her shoulder in an awkward self-conscious gesture. 'Mother – ' he said at last, in a voice which didn't sound like his own, and at the same moment his mother stepped back and sniffed and passed her hand over her eyes; she pulled her handkerchief from her sleeve and blew her nose. 'Time to be brave, darling,' she said. 'No more Daddy to look after us; we have to look after each other from now on . . . Can you do that?' she asked. 'Can you look after your poor old mum?'

He stared helplessly at her. 'You mean – now?' he said, finding nothing else to say. 'You mean instead of university and everything?' She was still beautiful, his mother, even though she'd passed forty earlier that year. The same fine blonde hair, though cut shorter now than when he was small; the same lovely dresses and jewellery, brooches, necklaces, ear-rings, bracelets; the same *Chanel* perfume, as intoxicating as ever. 'Darling, if you want to go to university, you can. Of course you can. You've earned it, after all. All I'm saying – '

She paused, looking at him with such concern on her face, such an imploring, vulnerable look, that he felt the tears springing into his own eyes. 'All I'm saying is, you don't have to go. Not if you don't want to. We can have a nice life together, darling. Just you and me. Nice clothes and things. Holidays abroad, if we want them. Outings together. A safe life. We shan't have to want for a thing.'

She reached out and laid her hand on his cheek: an old, familiar gesture. 'Of course you must go to university, if that's what you want. Of course you must. Only – ' and here her hand moved under his chin, tilting his head up so that he was looking straight into her eyes and she into his (such concern, such an intimate trusting look in her eyes!) – 'Only *is* it what you want, dear? Really and truly, I mean. I've had the feeling somehow that you're really not that keen on going. And now you don't have to. Like I said, we can have a really nice life together here – everything we want – '

He nodded, chewing his lower lip. It was a moment both shaming and liberating – for surely the shame would be forgotten before long? He'd said nothing to her about how he was dreading university, yet she still knew, had known even before he did, probably. She knew him better than he knew himself, just as she always had.

Impossible, of course, to foresee, nor did he for a moment stop to wonder, what looking after her might involve. The trips to Paris, Rome, Venice, Barcelona, where she would shop insatiably and he would trail behind her, a prim, tight-lipped little man, middle-aged while still in his twenties, walking with quick, nervous steps, carrying her purchases in brightly coloured boxes and carrier-bags. Her drinking, which would begin as 'enjoying a nice glass of wine now and then' and would escalate, in what seemed no time at all, to the point where she was never fully sober: her eyes dulled, face puffy and reddened through drink: sherries before lunch, cocktails before whatever slapdash inadequate dinner she'd prepared – she who had once cooked such lovely meals for him! – wine with dinner and another bottle after dinner, when the two of them would sit for hours in front of the television. Then out of nowhere the fits of rage, accusations that he didn't care about her, that he was 'feeble' – *If your father could see you! I just hope to heaven he can't!* – all of which he'd endure without ever once speaking back (and would never join her in drinking either, limiting himself to just a single reluctant glass of wine with his meal). Then in the kitchen one day she would slip and fall on the tiled floor, twisting her back, and despite all medical attentions would be in almost constant pain from then on, mixing painkillers with her drinks, dulling her body and mind still further. By then he'd be bringing her breakfast in bed each day, cooking for the two of them – or, rather, since he didn't know how to cook and lacked the confidence to try, attending to the heating-up of the ready-cooked meals he'd bought which tasted of nothing but were strangely comforting to eat every day. There was the paying of bills to deal with, his mother's money to keep track of – a task he dreaded, even though all the decisions regarding the money were made by the firm his mother had entrusted it to; there was the telephoning of tradesmen when they were needed, the shopping, the ferrying of clothes to and from the dry cleaners; every day there were things to be done, her tantrums to endure, her confusions, until finally he would help her up to bed in the evening, his arm round her waist, hers round his neck, her other hand hanging on to the banister, the two of them leaning on one another as if locked in that pose. Bringing her breakfast each day, he was fearful that soon the morning would come when there'd be no answer to his knock on her door. And then what? What purpose or meaning in his life? What justification for it? But then she'd call to him to come in and he'd set down her breakfast tray on the bed, plump up the pillows, take her napkin from its ring, kiss her cheek before leaving. Impossible to foresee any of this, and even if it had been possible, it would have made no difference. She was right, yet again. And she needed him now, for who else could she turn to with Daddy gone? She needed him and he would stay. It was what any good son would do, wasn't it, the very least he could do, for her and Daddy both.

Ice

Thirty-eight years ago – it was one raw, sunless day in
January 1966, in a city which I was to leave soon afterwards
and to which I have never returned – she and I took the bus
for several long miles across the city to the place where the
young man who not long before had been her lover was
buried. There'd been no one to claim his body, or to pay for a
funeral, none of us had given it a thought as far as I know, so
they'd buried him in the vast public cemetery reserved for
such cases: row upon row of tiny numbered crosses leaning
this way and that in the snow, stretching away almost as far
as we could see, and all she had was a slip of paper with the
number 34632 written on it. Just inside the gates of the
cemetery there was a small building with icicles hanging
from its gutters and ledges, where we hoped there'd be
someone who looked after the place and could tell us where
we'd find him; but it was closed up and empty-looking and
nobody answered when we pressed the bell. It was even

colder than usual for the time of year, the temperature freezing or lower, and beginning to fall now in the late afternoon. As we set off along one of several paths leading inwards from the gates, the wind stung our faces and the ice splintered with a harsh, angry sound under our feet. Then she called out from her side of the path that she'd found a cross numbered 33241, so perhaps we were close. I hurried over to her and we left the path and made our way with difficulty between the rows of crosses, stumbling on the uneven ground, sinking sometimes almost to our knees in the snow. We crossed another path, but then a different sequence of numbers began, starting with 19281, and we looked at each other unwilling to say what surely both of us were thinking: that this was all harder than we'd imagined, that we might search for ever without finding him among so many thousands. But we kept on looking anyway, moving at random from one path to another until we'd lost all sense of direction, both of us frozen by now as day turned to dusk. All I could think of was getting back to the warmth and safety of my apartment or, better still, to one of the many dimlit anonymous bars in the city, where it would be possible for a while to sustain the illusion that the world outside didn't exist. What difference would it make, anyway, if we found him? No difference to either of us, I thought, and most certainly none to him. It was a pointless and sentimental gesture, coming to look for him, and I was angry at having allowed myself to be talked into it, for having told myself, out of simple cowardice, that I didn't have any choice. But she wouldn't give in, I could see it in her face. I could see tears in her eyes again; I saw her biting her lower lip and in a frantic, crazed-looking gesture brushing at her face with the back of her gloved hand as she bent down to peer at yet another of those little crosses poking drunkenly out of the snow. Then she slipped and fell at the edge of the path and stayed there on her knees until I came and helped her back to her feet again. She leaned against me a while, shivering, then stood up straight and looked round wildly in the fading light. 'It's hopeless,' she said. 'Hopeless.' The tears ran down her face and I believe I hated myself more than ever then, because of the relief I experienced on seeing that she was finally going to abandon the search, as I would have abandoned it an hour or more ago when there'd still been at least a faint chance of finding him. I put my arm around her feeling that it was the most hypocritical act of my life and somehow we found our way out of the cemetery and back to the road and the bus-stop. Then we were sitting at the back of an almost empty bus, where she leaned her face into my shoulder and wept. 'It's all right,' I kept saying, though of course I knew it wasn't all right. It had ended between us, with his death. I'd wanted her as I'd never wanted anyone, with a passion that was like some vast and unbelievable force of nature sweeping me along, passion astounding and irresistible, beyond anything I'd known. I'd 'loved' her, I'd believed, had told her again and again that I loved her, and now as I sat with her body pressed against mine, her hair touching my cheek, the same body, the same hair, I felt nothing but this great cold impossible distance between us, as though we were figures far apart in some limitless expanse of ice and white sky at the very edge of the world. There was nothing I could say to her, and staring at my pale reflection in the window I thought of him lying there oblivious under the frozen earth. You bastard, I thought. Isn't this what you wanted? Haven't you won? As if I knew then, as if I could have known, that the landscape to which he'd brought us was the landscape where I was to live from now on, no matter where the years might lead.

Fall

Two years and eight months he's been on the wagon: ever since that New Year's Eve party where he drank excessively even by his own excessive standards and behaved not for the first time, though certainly in front of a greater number of people than ever before, in a crude and viciously destructive way that he flinches even now from recalling and that when his wife brings it up (as she still does from time to time, along with incidents of a similar if not quite so extreme nature, times when he was stupid, times when he was mean) makes him wish the ground would open and swallow him up. Now it's a hot August evening, quarter to seven, and he's sitting in a crowded pub in Soho waiting for a friend to arrive. They're supposed to meet here at seven, have a quick drink or two, then walk round the corner to a jazz club where the Negro pianist and singer, the 'legendary Georgia bluesman,' Jack McFee, is appearing. He's all right, sitting in the pub by himself, though he'd have preferred somewhere quieter and not so full as this place where every chair is taken, people standing three or four deep at the bar, the door constantly swinging open to let in yet more people; but still he's all right as far as not having a drink is concerned. It's been hot all day, and oppressively humid, more like the tropics than London; people must have poured into the pubs when they'd finished work, impatient, almost frantic, with the need for a cold beer, or for several cold beers. He can well understand that, even without feeling the need for one himself. There's a glass of mineral water with ice and lemon on his table, possibly the dullest drink in the world, he's often thought, but since he can't stand Coke and doesn't much care for fruit juice of any kind, mineral water's just about the only thing left to him. He's brought a paperback with him and there's no problem in just sitting here and reading until his friend arrives. But when after a while he glances up at the clock over the bar and sees that it's ten past seven, he knows suddenly that his friend isn't going to arrive. Just that feeling you sometimes get, *he's not coming,* only of course you can't actually be one hundred percent sure, so you keep waiting anyway, telling yourself he might be delayed at work or stuck in traffic or something, all the time convinced it's none of these things, just that your friend, so-called, has either forgotten or found something better to do. It isn't a close friend, in this case, just someone he knows through work and with whom he shares an enthusiasm for the blues, so he sits there reading and sipping his mineral water and then at half-past seven he decides he'll give it just five more minutes and he goes up to the bar with his empty glass and stands there for what seems an age while the barman serves a group of five girls who are giggling together, having trouble deciding what each of them wants. And when finally they've been given their drinks, and have rummaged in their bags for the money to pay for them, and the barman turns to him and asks does he want the same again, he says, 'No, a pint of John Smith's, please,' although right up to and even beyond the point of placing his order, he's had no thought at all of ordering anything alcoholic. But here it is now, and here he is, carrying it back to his table. He takes a long drink from the glass, thinking *first one in almost three years*, feeling at once angry with himself yet oddly relieved, as though some long and ultimately pointless ordeal has come to an end. The beer tastes wonderful, quenching a thirst he hadn't even realised was there, but he doesn't seem to want another one and when it's finished he leaves the pub and sets out through the narrow streets to the jazz club, five or six minutes away. One beer. It doesn't count for anything, he thinks; nor, come to that, does it count for anything that his friend hasn't turned up, he can enjoy Jack McFee just as well on his own as with someone else. The jazz club's in the basement of an office building and he goes down the steep flight of steps and tells the man at the door that he's booked and paid for a table for two but is here alone after all. The music hasn't begun yet and the club's almost empty, only three or four tables occupied. He's shown to a small table close to the stage but with a pillar next to it which it seems to him will block, or at least partially block, his view of Jack McFee. He calls a waiter over and, pointing out the obstruction, asks if he can be moved to a different table. But this can't be done apparently, not unless he wants to sit at the very back of the room from where there'll be several other tables between him and the stage. The only remaining table for two is already booked, and they can't give a table for four to just one person, it's against company policy. 'I am a member,' he says, trying to suppress his anger, and the waiter, who by his appearance and accent comes from one of the Mediterranean countries, says he's very sorry but there's nothing he can do. 'I don' make the rules,' he says, smiling almost intimately at him as if to assure him that they're both on the same side in this, both wanting the same thing and both powerless to get it. 'All right,' he says wearily, sitting down, 'okay, then.' He picks up the menu and studies it, though suddenly he doesn't really care what he has to eat and resents having to choose – there's almost nothing but pizza after all and the various toppings on offer aren't nearly as distinguishable from one another as the lists of ingredients on the menu would have one believe. The menu's nothing more than a confidence trick and he's not sure even if he feels like eating; he feels as full as if he'd eaten less than an hour ago, but he knows that if he doesn't eat he'll probably feel weak and unsteady later on, being one of those people who need a regular intake of carbohydrate, so he orders lasagne and a portion of garlic bread – and a bottle of mineral water he's about to add, but then as if eavesdropping on himself he hears, 'and a bottle of the house red, please,' the request surprising him just as that in the pub surprised him because again it wasn't the result of any conscious decision on his part but came out of his mouth as though of its own volition. The waiter pauses, pen poised over his order-pad: 'You wan' a half-bottle or a whole bottle?' he asks. 'A bottle, please,' he says. 'A whole bottle.' After the waiter's left, he lets out a long, slow breath which might be an expression of regret or of relief or perhaps simply of pleasurable anticipation, or perhaps all three, he can't tell and doesn't much care either, he realises. More people are coming into the club, a party of four now, and he looks at them as if from some hidden vantage-point where he's perfectly content to be alone, where the presence of anyone else at his table, whether they were known to him or not, would in fact be positively unwelcome. The waiter arrives with his wine and goes through the usual unnecessary ritual of opening it in front of him, asking if he wants to taste it before it's poured. He shakes his head, no, and watches while the waiter fills his glass almost to the brim; then he lights a cigarette and stares at the glass for a good five minutes before picking it up and drinking. It tastes as good as the beer did and almost immediately he feels it going to his head, bringing him to that bland almost anaesthetised state which before he went on the wagon it used to take him a bottle or even two bottles to reach. That abrupt loss of focus, that sense of life just dropping away somehow, even the most fearful and immediate difficulties just falling away, evaporating; he'd forgotten that feeling and wonders why he was never conscious of missing it during the last two-and-a-half years. He watches as Jack McFee comes from somewhere at the back of the club and, without any introduction or preamble, other than a faint nod and smile in acknowledgement of a scattering of applause, sits down at the piano, fiddles with the microphone for a few seconds and begins to play. He's been looking forward to this, having several of Jack McFee's recordings at home but never having heard him in person before. That great piano style, rolling chords, long inventive phrases which manage to go far away from the melody while still allowing it clearly to show, all the subtle little touches which lift Jack McFee several classes above your average blues pianist, though the blues, the feeling of the blues, are always there in his playing. This is what he's been waiting for, and for a minute or two – during which he discovers that by moving his chair a few inches he has an unobstructed view of the stage – it seems the evening's going to live up to expectations. But then Jack McFee hits a couple of wrong notes and he wonders if it's going to be a disappointment after all his hopes or whether, like many jazz or blues musicians, Jack McFee needs a few warm-up numbers before getting into his stride. When the music stops, he realises he's refilled and emptied his glass while McFee was playing. He fills it again, and lights another cigarette. The next number is the old *Trouble In Mind*, recorded by just about everyone over the years, and it becomes clear before long that, as he half-suspected, Jack McFee's no more than a shadow of the performer he was in his prime. There are more wrong notes and one barely credible moment when he loses the beat altogether and has to play a jarringly clumsy phrase to get back to it. Then when he sings he has trouble hitting the higher notes, hits them fractionally flat and in a thin reedy voice, not even a poor imitation of how he once used to sing. He's too old for this, and in fact looks too ill for it: a peculiar greyish tinge to his skin, his eyes bloodshot, a film of sweat on his forehead. *The legendary Jack McFee.* Better if he'd stayed a legend, given up performing and stayed back home in Georgia or wherever he lives. But that was never going to happen, of course, not with all those promoters and club owners wanting their money, and McFee himself probably needing it, none of them bothered for a moment if people feel let down, just as long as they've swallowed the bait and paid.

It's the same all over, isn't it? – people promising to meet you and not turning up, you give up booze and don't feel any better or even any different for it, pay way over the odds to hear some clapped-out old blues pianist. It's funny when you think about it, the way you go on nurturing these expectations, long after you should have learnt to know better. But that's how things are, he decides, the need for hope as fundamental as that for food and water and air, so that even when reason tells you there's no hope at all, or nothing worth hoping for, you go on hoping anyway. The wine's almost gone now, and when the waiter appears with his lasagne and garlic bread he pours the last half-inch into his glass and orders another bottle. Despite the impact of that first glass, he feels now as though he's just taken up where he left off all those months ago: the more you drink the more you want to drink and the more it's just like water you're drinking so that instead of slowing down you actually drink faster. ('If you could just have a glass or two and leave it at that,' his wife used to say – as if there was any point in having one or two glasses, as if it wouldn't be a hundred times harder to drink them and stop than simply to do without them.) His food tastes of nothing when he begins to eat, just 'food,' just 'something to eat,' of no noticeable texture or flavour as he chews and swallows. It strikes him as utterly bizarre all of a sudden, the way people sit cramming food into their mouths assuring themselves they're enjoying it because they're paying for it, the same as many of them, no doubt, having shelled out £15.00 to see Jack McFee, will tell their friends what a fabulous performer he is, what a fantastic evening they had. Now as the waiter brings his wine to the table and fills his glass, and gathers up the dishes from his table, it's nothing like anger or despair he's feeling at this cognizance of the way the world works; only a kind of amused, distant satisfaction, because he sees it all so clearly and because it seems to have nothing to do with him, he's not involved, not taken in for a moment. He thinks of his wife, how upset she would be if she could see him drinking in the same determined almost mechanical way as before, unable to stop once he's started until he's either asleep or there's no booze left. But so what, if she'd be upset? So what, if he has a hangover tomorrow? So what, if he won't be able to give up again? None of it matters. Not even his disappointment in Jack McFee matters, it belongs already to the past, as much a joke as everything else is. He's in some secure, locked-up place, from which he hardly even hears Jack McFee as he drinks. He's thinking of his wife again, remembering how only two or three weeks ago she said how happy she was to see he'd conquered his drinking problems; she'd doubted he could do it, she said, but he'd shown himself stronger than she'd thought. And now here he is, not merely proving her wrong but actually feeling good about it, thinking Serve you right for jumping to conclusions! as if his drinking again were some kind of triumph. Everything's so far away, the music, the sounds of people eating and drinking, talking, waiters moving about, it's like he's dreaming these things, or sitting in the dark watching a film, and he enjoys this sensation more than he's enjoyed anything in years, just being able to sit here and drink and not be touched by anything; and knowing, furthermore, that the booze won't run out, that if he wants anything more after this bottle he'll need only to catch the waiter's eye and ask for it. It's wonderful knowing there's at least *something* he can count on in this lunatic asylum of a world and that, because he can count on it, the question of whether it matters that it's all he can count on simply doesn't arise. But now he needs to pee and he gets up and threads his way among the tables to the gents, carrying his briefcase with him. This is good too, the relief of emptying his full bladder while knowing there's still damn near half a bottle of wine waiting for him back at his table. Yet as he leaves the gents he realises he wants to get out of this place; he's been here long enough, he decides, not exactly tired of being here but seeing no point to it, no point to prolonging an experience which doesn't really hold anything for him, it's time to get out and find somewhere else, he decides. So he doesn't go back to his table but, without hurrying, makes his way past the kitchen, past the bar and the manager's office and the admission desk, and on up the steps into the street. They've had his £15.00, of course, but he's had more than that back from them, two bottles of wine and a meal, probably about £30.00, he reckons: not feeling any great delight at having escaped without paying, or any need to justify it to himself, but pleased that he now has £30.00 to spend that he wouldn't otherwise have had, so that what-ever the rest of the evening might bring will in effect cost nothing. There's also some pleasure in thinking of all those people still left in the club, none of them with sufficient knowledge of what they're hearing to appreciate how truly awful Jack McFee's performance is. They've been robbed and they won't even know it, any more than will the thousands of others who'll pay to see Jack McFee during his much-publicised tour. It's this, not the fact that he avoided paying his bill, that makes him glad he got out. He's walking

without having any idea where he's headed, but when he
sees the lighted windows of a pub in front of him he pushes
the door open and goes up to the bar and orders a double
scotch. Ain't this the life! he's thinking, but the scotch is
gone almost before he knows it and he doesn't stay to order
another. It's too crowded and noisy and suffocatingly hot in
the pub, there's nowhere to sit, so he goes out into the
streets again to see what else he might find. The streets are
thronged with tourists, Americans and Japanese everywhere, and each of the three pubs he looks into is as packed
as the one he left. Then he turns a corner and sees on the
other side of the street, lit up like Christmas, the window of
an off-licence, row upon row of bright-labelled bottles, an
Aladdin's cave of booze, and as though hypnotised he crosses
the street and enters. 'A bottle of Teacher's, please,' he tells
the man behind the counter – so easy, so marvellously,
miraculously easy! – and then he's back on the street again
clutching the plastic bag with the bottle in it, keeping his
eyes open as he moves along for some place where he might
sit down and drink without having to put up with noise and
crowds and the necessity of keeping on going back to the
bar and waiting an age to be served – all those elements
which obstruct the real and only purpose of drinking, which
is simply to drink. Somewhere quiet, somewhere where he
can sit down and open his bottle and enjoy it in peace – this
is all he wants in the world right now, and when he spots a
narrow back-alley leading off the street he enters it and sits
down on the concrete path with his back against the wall
and opens the bottle and drinks. It's something like happiness he's feeling, an absence of care or concern that surely
is happiness. Not thinking of what time it is, or when or

whether he'll get home, or what his wife will say when she sees him drunk, or how he might feel when he wakes tomorrow – not thinking of any of these things, nor of anything else in the world, because there's an almost full bottle of scotch in his grasp and he suddenly laughs out loud as though he'll be sitting here with it for time without end, time and all other considerations fled and forgotten, fuck everybody!

Shot

Already it's evening again, six o'clock on a clammy evening in June, with some four hours of daylight remaining. You've left the office where you work, passed through the shopping centre, crossed the green in front of the council buildings, and reached the foot of the hill leading to the part of the city where your flat is located. There's not that much further to walk, three-quarters of a mile at most, but as happens so often at this point you feel an exhaustion so overwhelming that to take even one more step seems beyond you. Almost every day for seven years you've been climbing this hill. At first it was no trouble at all, was a pleasure even, because the city was new to you and seemed to hold out the promise of bringing significant encounters and momentous changes into your life. That was what had brought you here, after all, those were the promises you'd made yourself, founded on nothing more solid than what you wished and needed to believe. But the young man you were then changed long ago into the man you are now (or rather, remained the same man, but deprived of the capacity for hope) and when you remember how you once felt there's neither pain nor nostalgia involved, only a strange sense of distance and irrelevance, as if in fact you had never really been that young man. Long ago, you realised you'd been asking the impossible of the city, investing it with some extraordinary power through which, without any initiative on your part, it could change you into a different person. But what's the use of such insights? With or without them, your life is both what it was and what it will be, and perhaps this is the cause of your fatigue: not just the number of times you have climbed this hill, but the number of times you will climb it.

Here at the foot of the hill there's a dry cleaner's, an antique furniture shop and a French restaurant called 'Le Caveau' which has a good reputation in the city and which of course you have never visited. Outside 'Le Caveau', separating the forecourt from the pavement, there's a low brick wall with a few potted shrubs on it. You imagine yourself sitting down on this wall and not taking a step in any direction until, eventually, people come to take you away. You try to remember if there's anything to eat in your flat, because if there isn't you'll have to face the man in the corner-shop who always seems to look pityingly and complacently at you when you bring your few purchases to the counter, with a gleam of pleasure in his eyes which he either can't or doesn't want to conceal. You wonder if you should vacuum the carpets this evening, or wash out some clothes and hang them up to dry, or pass the hours just sitting in front of the television. (And, beneath these thoughts, the familiar question asserts itself, And then what? repetitive as everything else in your life.) But now you're walking again, leaving 'Le Caveau' behind, passing between rows of tall anonymous buildings with offices on their ground floors and either flats or more offices above. Perhaps some cars pass you, and perhaps some other pedestrians; you couldn't say, you've trained yourself not to notice other people, for fear you might see them noticing you back. Behind you, high on the roof of one of these buildings, there's a sniper taking a rifle from its case, the very latest kind of rifle with telescopic sights, such as you've seen used by assassins in films or TV shows. At first you decide he's been stationed there for the express purpose of killing you – someone's paying him to kill you, because of some crime you've committed. Then you realise this is stretching credibility too far, since you've never committed even the smallest crime, and certainly would never have been capable of a crime so important in its consequences that it would lead to someone ordering your death. You then decide that the assassin is being paid by no one, he's simply a psychopath who's got hold of a gun and is going to shoot someone for no better reason than that it will please him. You are walking up the hill, as slowly as you always walk; on the rooftop, the maniac has assembled his rifle, squinted through the telescopic sight and, after scanning the scene below, has focused perfectly on the back of your head. Any second now, his finger will squeeze the trigger.

You will feel nothing as the bullet penetrates your skull; you will fall and will be dead before you hit the ground or have had time to realise what's happened. People will gather round, believing you've collapsed because of a heart-attack or a stroke; then they will see the blood and some of them will cry out in shock or in terror; some will run away. Cars will pull up and more people will hurry to the scene, and none of it will matter to you. All that will matter is that you are dead and that it will not be your fault; no one will be able to blame you for having died, to say you died because you were too frightened and inadequate to carry on living. Then after the police cars and the ambulance have arrived, all the predictable questions will arise: Who were you? Where did you live? Who should be informed of your death? Somehow the police will find out the address of your flat and will enter it, to see what it might tell them about you. But there will be nothing. A few pictures on the walls, reproductions of famous paintings which long ago you cut out of magazines and which excited you for a while because it was only a matter of time, you believed, before they would be seen by others who would admire your taste and decide that, contrary to first impressions, you must be a person of interest. And a bookcase with two rows of paperbacks that will say nothing about you either. And some clothes in the wardrobe and the chest of drawers; some tins of food in the kitchen. Perhaps the police will search for a letter, or an address book, neither of which they will find. Those who witnessed your death will talk about it compulsively for a time; then they will talk about it only occasionally, and eventually they will cease talking about it; and you, stripped of all flesh and wearing only the bland smirk of the dead, will be past knowing, past caring.

Then

Twenty-seven years, since they saw each other last. And now here they are at noon this Saturday taking their seats in an Italian restaurant off Oxford Street, empty but for themselves.

It's incredible! the woman says. Twenty-seven years! Who would have thought it? Who would have dreamt it, even?

And you've hardly changed! she says, in a mock-envious voice, you certainly haven't changed twenty-seven years' worth! To which he replies – and means it, as he can't believe she does – that she hasn't changed much either. He recognised her voice on the phone, he tells her, though in fact he isn't sure whether it was before or after she told him who she was that her voice was so instantly familiar. But what does it matter? Her voice is the same anyway: that soft slightly husky voice, which *then* he'd found dizzyingly erotic, enough in itself to compel the most frantic desire, but which now suggests other qualities. A certain gentleness, he's decided; it's the voice of someone benevolent towards others, uncynical, interested. He's convinced of this, even while realising it's absurd to reach such conclusions about someone he hasn't seen for so long.

This is nice, she says. Looking round with visible pleasure at the framed Italian landscapes on the walls, menu chalked on a blackboard, bundles of dried flowers or herbs hanging from the ceiling. With each minute, and despite all outward signs of change, the feeling that she's still the same person he knew all those years ago grows stronger. Then, she was a tall willowy girl of twenty-one whose dark hair fell straight and shining to the small of her back, a girl with boyishly slim hips, a waist around which he could clasp his two hands, almost. Now her waist and hips have filled out, giving her an almost matronly figure, and her hair's cut short and is as much grey as black. And her clothes are different. Twenty-seven years ago, she'd favoured ski-pants and chunky sweaters and, outdoors, since it was winter at the time – winter in Montreal: snowfalls, sidewalks treacherous with ice, temperatures often way below zero – she'd worn a maroon corduroy coat, drawn tight at the waist but with extravagantly large lapels, in which she'd cut a brave flamboyant figure. He used to love that coat; more than anything she wore, it stood for everything in her that so beguiled and aroused him. No one else, he used to think, would have chosen such a coat, or been able to wear it with such an effortlessly rakish air. You look like a pirate, he used to joke, you should have an eye-patch and cutlass to go with that coat. Now she's wearing a loose-fitting dark-blue dress, almost ankle-length, dotted with small white flowers, and a grey-and-blue striped cardigan. Her clothes suit her; she wears them well, he thinks, in the manner of someone at ease with herself, at home in whatever she might be wearing.

But she's *the same person*, still. It doesn't matter about the clothes, or the figure, or the lines on her forehead, these aren't what count.

When he asks if this is her first visit to London, she says no, she's been here several times in the last few years. And she thought of phoning him each time, just looking him up in the phone-book and, if she found him, giving him a call. But she had no idea if he was living in London, or even in England, come to that; so much time had gone by! And then the impulse passed, or she was caught up with all the lectures and meetings she was required to attend, and in no time at all was flying back home.

Anyway, she says, laughing, it could have been the most humiliating anti-climax! I mean what if I'd called and you hadn't *wanted* to hear from me? What if you didn't *remember* me, dread thought!

But I did remember you, he says lightly. You were a memorable person. Still are, no doubt . . . His voice tails off, leaving unfinished whatever he might have said. It's necessary to be careful what he says, to keep a grip on himself. Better to say nothing, he's decided, than to let down his defences and risk saying too much.

When the waiter appears they order pasta dishes, a mixed salad to share, a bottle of red wine. She looks at him earnestly across the table and asks how he's been all these years. What's he been doing for a living? Is he married? Does he have any children? – all the questions he's known she would ask and has been dreading. Ever since she phoned, he's been trying to devise some strategy for dealing with them, evading them while appearing to answer them, saying nothing more than what needs to be said, without suggesting how much he chooses to leave unsaid. So now he tells her that he works for a publishing company and hopes that she takes this to mean some interesting 'creative' kind of job, when in fact he's on the sales side and the company he works for – situated not in bohemian Soho or literary Bloomsbury but in a 'business park' near Heathrow Airport – specialises in technical and medical books. And, yes, he's married and has two children, teenagers, a boy and a girl, and he lives in London. Which she knows, of course, though she certainly won't know the precise area where he lives. It's a dowdy unfashionable area, thirty-five minutes by tube from where they are now, where houses are cheap by London standards. It's an area where people often buy a house or flat as the first rung on the ownership ladder, but for him it's the last rung, he's there for good with his family, like it or not.

Her eyes shine as she listens to him. It must be wonderful, she says, living in London! Such character! Such diversity! All those theatres and concerts and art galleries to choose from, she really envies him all that. And there isn't any need, thank God, to tell her that he hasn't been to a play or an art exhibition for years now, he's become a person who thinks of art, when he thinks of it at all, as something with no point or relevance for people like him. Art angers him, in its irrelevance; though still sometimes he remembers the foreign films they used to go to together (especially he remembers that film they both cried at they were so moved, *Les Quatre Cents Coups*, with its marvellous closing sequence of the boy running towards the sea and then turning to face the camera, his face frozen, accusatory); he remembers the books they read and discussed, Brahms and Mozart and Bach on the record-player, or the blues singers so popular

then, Josh White and John Lee Hooker and Lightnin'
Hopkins, or sometimes Billie Holiday and Bessie Smith.

And a wife and two children! she says – admiringly, as if
the acquiring of a family was an achievement of some sort.
She'd love to meet them sometime, though she's sure it's
better this first time that only the two of them are meeting.
It would have been awkward probably, she says. Us trying to
catch up and everything, talking about things they wouldn't
know about. They'd feel . . . excluded, probably. She asks if
he has any photos she could see and he shakes his head, no.
He should have thought of this, the mutual showing of
pictures, almost obligatory in meetings of this nature, but
perhaps it was on purpose he overlooked it. There's nothing
especially attractive about his wife and children. He sees
them much as he sees himself: not exactly *un*attractive, but
certainly not in any way beautiful. Just un-noticeable, really:
anonymous people who travel on the tube every day, fret
over the cost of things, are not much given to laughter or
frivolity about the house, people who worry even when
there's no need because worrying's become so habitual as
to be almost addictive. It's not what you could call a
deprived way of living, but it wears you down, cuts you off
from things that might make life easier now and again. It
makes you wonder now and again just what might be the
point of such an enclosed, repetitive life.

It's fantastic to see you, he says, and she says You too! and
they touch glasses and drink. What about you? he asks, and
at once she's reaching down for the large straw bag beside
her chair and producing a wallet from which she removes
some pictures. Me and my husband, she says, and here she
is standing with a tall fair-haired man outside a white single-

storey house with flower baskets strung from the over-
hanging roof, a paved patio area with shrubs and climbing
plants. That's Dan, she says. We got married, oh, about two
years after you left, I guess. And this is Paul – now showing
him a picture of a young man also tall and fair-haired, but
slimmer, wearing jeans and a tartan lumberjacket, caught
squinting at the camera against a backdrop of water and
bright blue sky. He's twenty-three, she says proudly. Got his
master's this year and now he's going to travel for a year and
come back and work for his doctorate. I think he fancies
doing something in politics eventually . . . something radical,
she says with a grin.

She takes the photos from him and puts them back in her
bag. He doesn't like to think about her family, which seems so
superior to his. They must get on well together, he thinks, it
must mean something to them, being a family. And fairly
well-off – 'comfortably off' – enough money coming in so they
don't have to think about it too hard. When he asks what
work they do, she tells him Dan's a lecturer in modern
American literature – also, these last few years, engaged in
writing a fairly lengthy book on the subject – and she has
quite a high-up post in an organisation devoted to the study
of immigrant populations, particularly those from the more
'backward' countries, so-called, who have learning problems
or difficulties integrating with the indigenous population or,
more often, being accepted by it. That's why she's been in
London three or four times: to attend conferences, compare
notes, see how other countries are tackling these problems.
It's pretty hard work, she tells him, pretty frustrating at times.
But you do occasionally get the feeling you're accomplishing
something, that you're moving forward, if only by degrees.

She stops then, as the waiter puts down their food on the table, offers them parmesan and black pepper, says mechanically *Buon appetito!* before departing. The steam rises gently from their plates, giving off the odours of tomato and garlic and green peppers; she lowers her head towards her food, breathing them in. Great! she says. I think I'd die if I couldn't eat Italian food any more! Me too, he replies; though food, like so much else in his life, has lost all interest and appeal for him lately. One ate because one had to eat, just as one worked because one had to. His wife would call out that supper was ready and he'd sit down at the kitchen table and hardly notice what he was eating. Occasionally she'd complain that he never showed any enthusiasm for her cooking and he'd have to assure her that he'd enjoyed his supper, really he had, only he was a bit preoccupied right now. Preoccupied with what? she once asked, and he couldn't tell her. Preoccupation wasn't the word: it was a kind of lassitude that had descended on him, the feeling that irreparable mistakes had been made and their consequences would last for ever. Life's just gone by, somehow; he's made no choices, foolish or otherwise. Perhaps he's too passive a person even to have recognised the concept of 'choice'; and perhaps – more likely – it was simply easier that way, to submit to destiny rather than struggle to shape it. It might mean putting up with much one didn't like, and doing without things one would like; it might mean frustration and disappointment; but it was easier just the same, because it eliminated the need to struggle, the risk that you might struggle and fail anyway. The coward's strategy, is how he thinks of it.

. . . Johnny Morton, she's saying. You remember Johnny?

He's in California now, in the music business, we've gone down there and stayed with him a few times. And Sally? Sally Dempster? The name rings only the vaguest of bells, but Sally Dempster is now quite a prominent figure, it seems, having written a book on feminism followed by a novel about a lesbian love affair which has been translated into several languages and for which it's likely the movie rights will be sold. And Dave Germiston, who married an American girl, lives with her and their children on the coast of Maine and has his own boatyard – remember Dave? A sort of spasm seizes him as she tells him this, something twisting his guts, a pain so sudden and intense that it's all he can do to stop himself crying out. He gets up carefully from his chair, telling her he'll be back in just a moment. At the back of the restaurant, behind the door marked TOILETS, a steep flight of stairs leads down to a basement; halfway down he experiences another stab of pain and this time he does gasp, hanging on to the banister and forcing himself to breathe slowly until the pain lessens. Then he's in the lavatory, sitting in a dim-lit cubicle with a rusting old-fashioned cistern above his head, between walls crowded with graffiti. Relief comes instantly: a relaxing of muscles, shit pouring out of him as if at the turning on of a tap; pain, and the threat of pain, ended in moments. He's survived, he's got through this crisis, and if at the back of his mind there's the thought that 'getting through' is the best he's ever going to manage, he's too thankful to care right now.

He washes his hands, staring at himself in the chipped fly-specked mirror. Twenty-two, he was then, and now he's forty-nine: of course he's changed! And yet she said he hadn't changed, and she surely wasn't the sort of person who'd say something just for politeness' sake? Perhaps it's only in his own dark perception of himself that he looks so bad, perhaps he's been doing himself an injustice. Hasn't it happened occasionally that, on learning his age, people have expressed surprise? Hasn't his own wife told him he looks younger than he is? Yes, more than once she has, yet it isn't so much the physical signs of ageing he sees in the mirror as evidence of what might be considered its emotional penalties: a look of fatigue and resignation in the eyes, of bafflement, as if already his life's nearing its end and he doesn't understand how or why any of it's happened and why he's drawn so little satisfaction from it. Often he's thought that this must be the first thing people see when they look at him, a dazed, beaten face.

But she phoned him, didn't she? It isn't as if they've met on his initiative, or run into one another by chance. She'd gone to the trouble of searching for him in the phone-book, must have been hoping to find him. What did that mean? Why, if she's as happy as he's assumed she is, would she have bothered? And why, if it comes to that, should she see in him only what he imagines people to see? Perhaps he's wrong. Perhaps people don't see him at all as he imagines them to.

Perhaps there's – something, after all? Something more than just curiosity; perhaps affection, even. Perhaps, for reasons he couldn't be expected to know, some dissatisfaction with her own life, her own marriage –

He smiles as he makes his way back to the table. Sorry about that, he says casually, sitting down. He keeps his eyes on her as she talks, but his mind's elsewhere, swinging pendulum-like between 'then' and 'now' as though 'then' were no further behind them than yesterday. It was his fault they'd split up: she'd gone home for Christmas, back to her parents' home in Ontario, and while she was gone he'd slept not once but several times with a girl who was supposedly her close friend. And then she'd come back again and the two of them had confessed, and that had been the end of it. By then he'd stopped feeling anything at all for her, so that her pain, her anger, had merely irritated him, filling him with an overwhelming desire for escape. Soon afterwards he and the other girl had gone to Toronto together, where it had quickly become apparent that they felt nothing much for one another either, and not long after that (still to his profound mystification and regret) he'd chosen to return to England. But it hadn't *had* to be like that. If he'd repented and thrown himself on her mercy begging for one more chance, if she'd understood that he'd been angry with her for preferring her family's company to his and had acted as much in revenge as anything else (as indeed the girl had acted, resenting her role as the less desirable, less intelligent of the two of them) – if he'd been able to explain all that to her, and she'd understood and forgiven him, they might have stayed together and loved each other even more. And now as they sit here waiting for their coffee to cool, he feels suddenly that it isn't too late, life's been awful all these years, but that doesn't mean it has to be awful for good, surely? She's found him again, and here they are talking as casually and easily to one another as if they've never been apart.

She phoned *him*: that's what counts, isn't it? Just like him, she might have looked back over the years and regretted their parting, wishing she hadn't reacted as she had, thinking if only she'd had the foresight to get through that crisis and stay with him. All it needs, perhaps, is for one of them to find the courage to say something.

He waits until she's paused in her talk and a few seconds of silence have passed. Then, though sweaty with apprehension and feeling suddenly as though this entire encounter is a dream, he says:

I often think about it, you know. About those days, I mean. The life we had then.

So do I, she says, smiling. It's strange, really. The older I get the more I seem to think about it. I guess that's what it's like for most people when they feel middle-age coming on.

She sips her coffee, a meditative look in her eyes. She smiles faintly. It's crazy, what he's thinking. He's forty-nine years old, more than half his lifetime has passed since they were together, and now it's suddenly only his family he can see, Caroline and Lorna and James, the three of them sitting silent and unmoving in the kitchen, heads bowed, as though in submission to some unavoidable blow. It does something to him, seeing them sitting there like that; the phrase *pivotal moment* takes root in his head, as if already the time has come when he's going to enter the kitchen and tell them he's leaving, he doesn't want them any more. But could it be done? Could he find it in himself to hurt them that much? to disrupt his own life that much?

He brushes the questions aside, picking up the bottle and pouring what's left of the wine into their glasses. It was a good time, he says. A happy time. Just a shame it ended as it did.

Yes, it was a shame, she says. But then again –

He waits. He feels he's trembling as he sits there waiting to see what she'll say.

I guess it's like childhood, really. I mean, that's how I think of it – those years between twenty and twenty-five when you think you're grown up, but in fact you're not. All we were, really, was children with a sex-drive, children who thought their childhood had ended.

He laughs, somehow; tells her somehow that, yes, she's probably right.

She leans towards him, laying her hand on his. Listen, it *was* a good time. Really it was. We have to be glad for times like that. We have to look back and be grateful, because there really aren't that many good times, when you think about it.

He nods, his throat too tight to permit speech. Whatever he might have foreseen of their meeting, it certainly wasn't this – that she'd see through him so easily, see everything he'd resolved to keep hidden –

There are people who've never had *anything*, she says. Really lonely people out there. Nothing to look back on, even. Not a time in their lives.

Yes, I know. I know there are.

And you have your wife and children! You've worked for them, given them a home! She looks at him with a pained, puzzled expression. That counts for a lot, you know. It's not something anyone can do.

No, I know. I know it isn't.

The waiter brings their bill and he picks it up quickly from the tray, waving aside her protests. No, it's on me, he says. I insist.

You're sure? she asks.

Yes, I am. Really. It'll be my pleasure to pay.

Well, thank you, she says, with a little bow of her head. Next time it'll be my turn.

There's an awkwardness now between them. He occupies himself with fishing his credit card out of his wallet and handing it to the waiter with the bill. I've really enjoyed this lunch, she says. It's great to see you're doing well for yourself, to see you've made something of your life.

Her voice softens. Those middle-age blues, she says. I'm afraid we all get them. I know I do, sometimes.

He smiles again; there's nothing much for it but to smile. That's right, he says. Intimations of mortality, I suppose.

Outside again, they walk back through the streets and down the steps into the tube-station. I wish we could have had longer, she says, as they reach the ticket-gates. But – well, you know how it is. So much to do, so little time! At the top of the escalator she turns, pauses a moment, then kisses him on the cheek. Listen, you take care now, she says. You look after yourself.

You too. And if you're back again ever –

Oh, I'll look you up, she says, laughing. And I'll buy lunch next time. You can count on it.

He stands there watching while the escalator carries her down. When she steps off it she turns and gives him a smile and a wave. Then she's gone and there's just this awful desolation sweeping down on him: the lies he's been telling all these years: the deceits, the evasions. The people hurrying past him have a distant unreal quality; all the sounds around him merge into a single sound and he wonders for a moment if he's going to fall, or faint, from what he's feeling. It's too much to bear, it would be too much for anyone, wouldn't it, to be feeling like this?

He crosses the foyer, goes down the escalator to the Piccadilly Line, and stands on the platform and waits. Next train, Rayners Lane, 4 minutes, he reads on the indicator. Years have sped by, almost without his noticing, and now these four minutes stretch ahead of him like a lifetime. He sits down on an empty bench, pressing his hands against the sides of his head, looking down at his knees. He notices how worn the knees of his grey corduroys are and how the cuffs of his jacket are starting to fray. He recalls how his face had looked when he stood staring at it in the restaurant lavatory. It must have been pity she felt for him, surely? – or was it more triumph than pity, seeing how he who had betrayed her had made so little of himself, was leading so thankless a life? She must have been glad she'd got in touch, it must have left her feeling better than ever about herself.

The train arrives and as he enters it and sits down, the desolation fades and a sudden raw rising anger takes its place. What do they know, anyway, she and her husband? A subsidised do-gooder and a subsidised academic: hard to imagine a more cosseted existence, hard to imagine they'd have the faintest knowledge of lives like his own, or care about them, or ask themselves if they should care. It's the way of things, isn't it? – all those people who'd be the first to profess that they 'care,' that they're 'involved,' all of them separate and safe from the forces which govern most people's lives – safe from life itself, in effect. It's ideas they're involved with, reality is for him and his kind.

In one thing only was she right: that it counted for something, looking after a family. The responsibilities of it, the things one had to give up; she was right about that, even though it was no more than a formulaic observation, thrown to him as one might thoughtlessly toss a scrap of food to a dog, and she probably didn't even know she was right. He

wishes she was with him still, so he could tell her yes, he
lives in the real world, lives daily with real hardships, real
anxieties. Not a world she'd want to live in, that's for sure.
Probably not a world she could live in, even if she did
want to.

He's close to the limit on his credit card after paying for
lunch, but opening his wallet he finds three tenners and a
fiver in it. Enough to take Caroline out somewhere this
evening, he thinks, perhaps a film and a curry afterwards,
like they used to on a Saturday night. Caroline will say, But
I've already cooked for this evening, and he'll say, Don't
worry about it, we'll eat it tomorrow. He won't take no for an
answer because his wife deserves to be taken out – deserves
more than just the local cinema and curry-house, deserves
more than he's ever been able to give her. He thinks, *It'll
cheer her up a bit* and suddenly there are tears in his eyes.
I'm sorry, he hears himself say, as clearly as if he's said it out
loud. The train hurries him back through the dark. He passes
the back of his hand across his eyes, sees himself ordering
curries for the two of them, raising his glass of beer to his
wife, looking into her eyes as into the eyes of a lover.

Pill

At ten that evening Stewart swallowed one of his sleeping-pills, rinsing it down with the day's last cup of decaff. He would have taken a pill every evening, only he was scared that if he took them too often he might develop a resistance to them that would stop them working. He was also scared that if he went back too soon to ask for more the doctor would refuse to give them to him because he'd be worried about Stewart becoming addicted. He limited himself to one pill every three or four weeks, saving them for those evenings when he felt he just couldn't face another bad night. Zopiclone, they were called, and they were far from the strongest pills on the market. But they were strong enough, the doctor had told him, and they wouldn't have any unpleasant after-effects. And this was true, more or less. He always had a dry mouth the next morning, and his body behaved in a sluggish and unresponsive manner, but never for more than an hour or two.

Tonight his wife Jenny had gone to her evening class, where she was taking a course on the history of art. She and a few others in the class had been asked back to someone's house for drinks afterwards, so it would probably be midnight or later when she came home. He'd be sound asleep by then, which would be better than having to pretend to be asleep, as he usually did when she came in late. Sleep was all he wanted, and it was nice to be getting into his pyjamas knowing he would sleep. It was the nicest feeling available to him, he often thought, though when he looked back to when he was twenty-five or so he realised that if anyone had told him it would come to this, he'd have been unable to take them seriously. He thought often about his past, the places he'd lived in, the girls, the escapades, the friends he'd had when he was young. But it wasn't painful, strangely enough. It was like turning the pages of a photo album, only somehow it wasn't his album, the pictures in it had nothing to do with him. He knew this was probably the result of some unconscious defence mechanism operating; but the alternative, he felt, would be to go crazy, to lose control in some way, and the consequences of losing control were frightening to contemplate. Sometimes he wondered if he'd just break down and cry, but there were other times when he saw himself throwing furniture about or smashing windows or even attacking his wife. This was something he tried not to dwell on: the idea that there was another self inside him, perhaps even his 'true self,' if there was such a thing, whose capabilities couldn't be guessed at.

He thought of his past with neither pleasure nor regret, but he'd become increasingly preoccupied with it lately. Perhaps it was precisely *because* it didn't seem real that he couldn't leave it alone – as if one day his thinking would trigger some response that would bring it, and himself, back to life again, restoring the person he had become to the more eager and responsive person he had been. But more likely, he thought, it was just a convenient way of avoiding the present. His thoughts were always the same, always seemed to end where they'd begun and then, set off by he didn't know what, begin again from the same spot all over. It was exhausting always to be following the same circular path, but he could find no way out of it.

*   *   *

He sat up in bed and took the alarm-clock from the bedside table and wound it. Seven o'clock, it was set to ring. Usually he slept about four or five hours a night – interrupted hours as often as not, because he'd keep sleeping and waking and sleeping again. It was only a half-sleep and often it was filled with wild and indecipherable dreams from which he woke in a bruised, edgy condition. Occasionally there were mornings when he'd wake about five, then fall asleep again and miss the alarm. Then when he did wake up he had to rush to get to work on time. He hated that. To have a lousy night and then to have to rush in the morning put him in a resentful, irritable mood which he couldn't shake off for hours.

Other men, he thought, or most other men, would be woken by their wives in the morning. But Jenny worked part-time, and locally, from eleven till four. There was no need for her to get up when he did, and she slept so deeply that she never even stirred when the alarm rang. Nor did they have any children to wake up and get off to school. They'd tried for children and failed. They'd considered adopting for a while, but had come out against it. You never knew, with adoption. You never knew who you were getting or where they came from, and if you wound up with a difficult or unlikeable child there wouldn't even be the tie of blood to help see you through. That was how both of them felt, or claimed to feel; though occasionally, before he'd stopped thinking about the subject altogether, Stewart had wondered if they really hadn't wanted any children. Anyway, it was all too late now. He'd be forty-two next month, and the month after Jenny would be thirty-nine. It wasn't literally too late, but it was in every other sense. He worked full-time and Jenny worked part-time, filling her free hours with a variety of activities. She visited art galleries and museums a great deal. She read the books recommended by her evening class teacher. She belonged to a reading-group, herself and four other women who each month picked a novel to read and then met to discuss it, and she was friends with a number of local potters and painters, all of them women, whom she spoke of as 'interesting' or 'exceptionally talented' and whose work was displayed from time to time in obscure little galleries in the area. She liked to visit her friends, or to meet them in one of the many local restaurants or wine bars. This was her life, and Stewart would have accepted it more easily if not for the fact that she had abandoned all the mundane but necessary tasks that were also meant to be part of her life. Regularly he came home from work to find that she was out somewhere, had left a pile of washing-up in the sink and had prepared nothing for supper. Twice recently it had been raining when he'd come home and there'd been clothes hanging on the line in the back-garden which he'd had to bring in and drape on radiators or over the banisters. It annoyed him that she seemed to consider these tasks too trivial to be worth bothering with: beneath her, but not beneath him, apparently. But then he'd fry some eggs or heat up some soup and his anger would disappear. When he'd finished eating, he'd light a cigarette and read the paper. He'd wash the dishes and put them away, which enabled him to feel virtuous and hard done by without taxing him too much. It was all right, being alone. It was actually quite pleasant, and lately when he'd come home to find the house empty he'd found himself listening with apprehension for the sound of his wife's key in the door.

*   *   *

He reached for his glasses and put them on, then picked up the book he'd brought upstairs. It was a book taken at random from the shelves, a collection of stories by Ernest Hemingway. All he needed was to have something to look at, to focus on, for those few minutes before the pill took effect. It had nothing to with reading in the way he once used to read. He opened the book and flipped back through the pages until he came to the beginning of a story. *In the fall the war was always there but we did not go to it any more.* He read to the end of the page, and to the end of the second page. Then when he was halfway through the third, he felt himself beginning to go. The words swam as he looked down at them, and he had to blink several times to bring them back into focus. He reached the end of a paragraph and couldn't recall any of it but the last sentence, and then that too disappeared. These were the signs he was familiar with and welcomed. He put down the book on the bedside table, took off his glasses and laid them on top of the book.

He switched off the lamp and closed his eyes and felt himself losing all sense of his weight, his being. He pictured himself being lifted by angels and lowered on to a soft mattress of clouds.

*   *   *

It was a banging noise that woke him. At first he heard it without really knowing he was hearing it. Then he identified it: someone knocking, somewhere. Then he realised it was someone knocking at his own front door.

Jenny, he thought. Jenny had forgotten her keys when she'd gone out. He got out of bed, shuffled into his slippers and pulled on his dressing-gown. He looked at the luminous dial of the alarm-clock and saw that it was ten to eleven, only fifteen or twenty minutes had passed since he'd fallen asleep. His legs felt weak, as if he were getting up for the first time after illness. He moved slowly, holding on to the banister as he went downstairs.

When he switched the hall light on, a face appeared at the small window by the front door. It was Gavin, who lived across the street at number 47. Gavin waved at him wildly through the window and Stewart opened the door. 'Hi,' he said, blinking, and Gavin said, 'Christ, you're in bed, Stewart. I didn't think you would be, at this hour.' He grinned, swaying slightly, then reached out an arm to the door-jamb to steady himself. 'Yeah, thought I'd have an early night for once,' Stewart said. He was awake enough to recognise that Gavin was drunk. He'd never particularly liked Gavin, primarily because Gavin seemed so much to like himself, but at the moment he had no feelings for him of any kind. He didn't even feel angry at having been woken up. He'd taken a sleeping-pill and its effects wouldn't have worn off by the time he got back to bed. The only thought in his head was that, whatever happened, he mustn't let on to Gavin that he took sleeping-pills sometimes. This was all that mattered and he was concentrating hard on remembering it.

'Stewart, listen,' Gavin said. 'Reason I knocked. Thought I might drag you back to Dave and Jan's house with me. They've got some people in – Larry and Isobel and a few others. Impromptu party sort of thing.'

'I think I'll pass,' Stewart said. 'I need a few hours' sleep, to tell the truth.' His voice echoed back at him as he spoke, as though it belonged to someone else. It had a remote, sepulchral sound.

'Oh, come on,' Gavin said. 'It's only a few doors away, for God's sake! Bung some clothes on and join us. It's been ages since we had a drink together.'

'I can't,' Stewart said. 'Really I can't.' He paused, giving Graham a consciously serious look. 'I'm too tired, right now.'

Gavin waved his arm in a dismissive back-handed gesture, like someone swatting away a fly. 'Course you're not! Course you're not too tired, man! Come as you are, if you like. It'd be a laugh, coming in your pyjamas and dressing-gown. Don't be a party pooper!'

'Not tonight,' Stewart said doggedly. 'I have to get some sleep.'

Gavin shook his head. 'Well, who would have thought it? Stewart Addison too tired to come to a party. What are things coming to?'

He came closer to Stewart and Stewart smelled the beer on his breath. 'You're not feeling ill or something, are you?' Gavin asked, an exaggerated look of concern on his face.

'Just tired,' Stewart said.

'Okay,' Gavin said. 'All right, then. We'll let you off this time. But, listen, we'll have a session in the pub sometime soon. Catch up on things. Okay?'

'Sure,' Stewart said. 'Fine.'

'Good,' Gavin said. 'I'll give you a shout one evening. Sometime next week, maybe.'

'Fine,' Stewart said. 'I'll look forward to it.'

'Stewart Addison in bed by half-past ten.' Gavin grinned at him, looking into his eyes, then reaching out and gripping him by the elbow. 'You take care now,' he said in an earnest 'sincere' voice which wouldn't have fooled a child. 'You get back to bed and catch up on your beauty sleep.'

'Thanks,' Stewart said. He watched Gavin make his way through the eight or ten yards of front garden, then unlock the gate and turn left towards Dave and Jan's house. They lived about fifty yards away, on the other side of the road, and just before Stewart closed the door he saw Gavin lurch to one side as he stepped off the pavement, in a way that made him think of a ship suddenly listing.

He turned the hall light off and went back upstairs. In the bedroom he took off his dressing-gown and hung it on the back of the door and shook off his slippers. The bed was warm when he got in. He turned on his side and pulled the duvet up to his chin.

*   *   *

There was a door slamming, and seconds later when he opened his eyes he had to close them again at once because the main bedroom light was on. Then he opened them more slowly and saw Jenny standing over him.

Jenny sat down hard on the bed. 'Hi, how's it going?' she said – casually, as if she'd come home to find him sitting in the living-room or the kitchen. She rummaged in her bag and pulled out cigarettes and a lighter. 'So,' she said, in an emphatic, businesslike tone. She lit her cigarette and blew out a stream of smoke. 'Shit,' she said, looking round, 'no ashtray.' They'd decided long ago that the bedroom would be a non-smoking zone, but now she looked at Stewart and said, 'You couldn't go down and get one, could you? I'm a bit – tired.'

Stewart got out of bed again and put on his slippers and went downstairs to the kitchen. When he returned, Jenny had taken off her shoes and was lying on the bed smoking in a languid and over-elaborate manner, like an actress over-playing the part of someone who smoked. She took the ashtray from him and balanced it on her stomach. 'So what's new?' she said. 'What's been happening?'

'Nothing,' Stewart said. He lay down alongside her, pulling the duvet up over his chest.

'Nothing,' Jenny repeated. She shrugged. 'Well, of course,' she said. 'What other answer could there be? When was the last time anything actually *happened* around here?' She sat up, knocking the ashtray to one side and catching it just before it fell. 'Oh my God,' she said, brushing the spilled ash off the duvet. 'Look at that. Something almost happened there, for a moment. My God.'

She looked scornfully at him. 'You know why nothing happens round here? Because you don't *want* anything to happen. That's why.' She glowered at him, pulling down her mouth in a caricature of disgust. 'It's sad,' she said, shaking her head. 'You're a very sad person.'

Stewart didn't answer. Jenny lay on the bed smoking for a

while, then got up and went to the window. She pulled the curtain aside and stood with her back to him, looking out into the dark, turning her head first one way then the other, as if expecting someone she knew to arrive. She seemed far away, as though the bedroom had suddenly expanded to several times its size. Stewart felt he was an absolutely minute being lying in bed. It was how he'd felt as a child sometimes: looking down on himself from some immense height, feeling as freakishly tiny as Tom Thumb under the vast expanse of the bedclothes.

'So nothing's happened, then,' Jenny said. 'Nothing whatsoever's been going on.' She turned away from the window and puffed at her cigarette in the same exaggerated manner as before, her other hand on her hip. She was swaying slightly and then she tottered forward, bringing her foot down hard on the carpet. 'Shit,' she said.

'Something did happen,' Stewart said. 'Gavin came and knocked on the door.'

'What?' Jenny stood stock still, halfway in the act of bringing her cigarette to her lips. 'Gavin from across the road? This evening?'

'That's right. Wanted me to come with a party with him.'

Jenny became suddenly alert. 'What party? Where? You mean it's going on right now?'

'Dave and Jan's house. They asked him and he knocked on the door and asked me.'

'What about me? Did he ask if I was in?'

'I think he knew you weren't. There weren't any lights on.'

'And he didn't ask where I was?'

'Not that I remember,' Stewart said.

Jenny picked up the ashtray from the bed and put out her

cigarette. 'Maybe I should go there. What d'you think?'

'Dunno,' Stewart said. 'Not for me to decide.'

'I know that,' Jenny said sharply. She took out her cigarettes again and spent several seconds trying to light one, waving the lighter too far away from it. 'What d'you think, though?' she said, giving up. 'Should I go or not?'

Stewart closed his eyes. 'If you want to, you should,' he said, after a while. 'If you don't want to, you shouldn't.'

'It might be fun,' Jenny said. 'I haven't seen Gavin for ages. Or Dave and Jan.'

She stood there frowning, pursing her lips, as if pondering some problem of enormous complexity. 'Maybe I'll just go for an hour or so,' she said. 'Just to say hallo. What d'you think?'

'Go by all means,' Stewart said, 'if it's what you want.'

'Yes. I will go,' she said. 'It might be fun, seeing them all for a while.' She sat down on the bed and picked up her shoes and put them on. 'You don't mind? You don't think it's stupid or anything?'

'No.' Stewart raised his arm in a vague benedictory gesture and almost at once let it fall. 'Have a good time,' he said, sinking back on the pillow. 'Give them all my regards.'

He felt Jenny's hand running through his hair, her lips brushing his cheek. 'I'll see you later then,' she said, in the affected intimate tone she often used when they were parting. 'Have a good sleep, now,' she said. As she reached the doorway, she said, 'I'll say hallo to everyone for you. Okay?' Then the light went out and she was gone. Stewart waited to hear the front door closing, then turned on his side and drew up his knees.

*   *   *

He never dreamed, or certainly had no dreams he could remember, when he'd taken a pill. But now he was dreaming. There were voices, in the dream. A man's voice. A woman's voice. There was a sudden crashing sound, and then the woman's voice crying out: 'Shit! Shit shit shit! Shit!' It was a wild, almost hysterical voice and Stewart recognised it as Jenny's. Then there was the man's voice again – Gavin's. 'You're okay, Jenny. You're all right. Just try and get up now.' More bumping and crashing noises, then Jenny's voice saying something he couldn't catch.

'Jenny, please,' Gavin's voice said. 'Listen to me. Where d'you want to sleep? In bed or downstairs on the sofa? How can I help if you won't tell me?'

Stewart lay in bed listening. It was interesting suddenly and the craving for sleep had disappeared. Tomorrow he'd ask Jenny how the party had gone, then ask her what time she'd got home and see what she said. It would be interesting because he'd know it had been twenty-five past three when she'd come in and she wouldn't know he knew. She'd lie to him, not dreaming for a moment he knew the truth.

There was more noise, a sort of scrabbling sound this time. Then: 'I'm okay,' Jenny's voice said. 'I'm okay. I'm fine.' But she sounded far from okay. She sounded like someone drunk to the point of near-incoherence, and certainly too drunk to be able to make it up the stairs on her own, or even to stay on her feet. Stewart lay there enjoying the fact that they were assuming he was asleep. It gave him a feeling of power, of superiority, to be listening without their knowing it.

'Go home!' Jenny's voice said fiercely. 'Go home, Gavin! Please! Leave me! I'm all right! I don't need you, thank you!'

'Jenny, listen – '

'Go home! Leave me! I don't need your help! *Just – leave – me – alone!*'

'Jenny, I can't leave you. Just tell me where you want to go. I'll help you get there.'

There was another crash, presumably the result of Jenny trying to get up again, to prove she didn't need any help. 'Oh!' Stewart heard her cry out.

'Jenny, listen to me,' Gavin's voice said. 'Just tell me where you want to go. I'll get you there. Are we going upstairs or d'you want to sleep downstairs on the sofa? Just tell me, please.'

'I don't care. I'll sleep here. Just – just – '

'Jenny, you can't sleep on the stairs. Don't be ridiculous. I'll take you back downstairs, if you like. You can lie down on the sofa and sleep it off.'

'No,' Jenny's voice said. 'Don't want to sleep on the sofa. Sleep in the spare room.' 'Right,' Gavin's voice said. 'Okay, then. We'll get you there. Which door is it?'

'Top of the stairs. Strai' 'head of you.'

Stewart heard what he assumed were the sounds of Gavin getting Jenny on her feet again and manoeuvering her up the stairs. Every few seconds Jenny made a loud grunting noise, as of someone exerting a terrific effort, and once Gavin's voice said, 'It's okay, pet. You're fine. I've got you.' After this there was silence for a while. Then there was Jenny's voice again: 'Gavin, no! No, Gavin! No!' And Gavin's voice, now only partially audible: 'Jenny . . . saying back there . . . remember . . . you said . . . ' The sound of a door opening. The sound of something, or someone, falling, and then the door closing again. Stewart sat up in bed, listening harder. 'Don't fight it, Jenny,' he heard Gavin say. 'Come on,

now.' 'Gavin, I shouldn't. We mustn't.' 'Don't be silly, Jenny.
You know perfectly well.' 'Gavin, no. We shouldn't. We
can't.' 'But you want to, Jenny. You know you want to.'

For several minutes after this there was nothing to hear
except vague scuffling noises and words Stewart couldn't
make out, whispered words which nevertheless had a quality
of urgency about them. Then he heard Jenny making sounds
which, even though it was an age since he'd heard them, he
recognised at once. They began as a deep moaning noise
which, gradually at first, but then more swiftly, rose in
volume and pitch and ended in what was almost a scream –
that sound which to his ears had always in recent years had
a harsh, theatrical quality, more suggestive of rage than of
pleasure. At the same time, he could hear Gavin making
noises whose meaning was equally unmistakeable, and he
could hear the bedsprings creaking. The sounds diminished
and ceased, and not long afterwards he heard footsteps
moving downstairs and the front door closing. He wondered
if Jenny had consented to what had happened, or if it had
been a case of Gavin moving in on her when she was too
drunk to resist. But he didn't wonder for long. There was
silence now and he was grateful for that. He'd been wide
awake a few minutes ago, but now his eyes were closing
again and his body was becoming as numb and weightless as
before. Nothing else mattered to him but to fall asleep, even
though there were now only three hours left before the alarm
would ring. He would sleep now, and so what if he missed
the alarm? He was abandoning himself so voluptuously to
sleep that he couldn't have cared less.

Warmth

Prep school. Smells of cabbage and small boys' bodies in the hall; the pegs where they hang up their caps and raincoats (A.'s is number twenty-seven, the same as his toy locker and washroom peg and games-clothes locker in the changing-room); then the shoelockers and the gloomy little alcove under the stairs where Riley the dark-faced odd-job man often stands polishing the boys' shoes.

It's here in the hall, as the boys queue outside the dining-room waiting to be let in to supper, that there's the sound of the door to the staff room opening and A. hears Major Baxendale calling his name. 'Remember your extra maths this evening, my child. You may come to me at twenty past seven, after your bath.' Then the door closes again and the boys resume their chattering and jostling.

My child. None of the other masters ever uses that expression. They call the boys by their surnames, or in rare and unconvincing attempts at informality by whatever nickname the boy they're talking to has acquired: Bish, Barrel, Greedy-guts, Froggie . . .

The Major had served in India before taking up teaching: a brisk, wiry little man, grey moustache, thinning grey hair, his blazer daubed with white where he's carelessly let cigarette-ash or chalk-dust fall. Unmarried, he lives at the very top of the school, above the dormitories, with his own bathroom and lavatory. As if (which later in life A. wants to believe but can't) the powers that be knew of his predilections and rather than risk scandal and perhaps even closure by taking action against him, had placed him as far from themselves as possible and closed their eyes.

A. enters the Major's room to the sound of the gas-fire sputtering, the smell of toast and cigarettes. On the walls there are several framed photos of soldiers in shorts and what A. thinks must be pith-helmets. The Major squats in front of the fire with his toasting-fork. 'Hot buttered toast,' he says over his shoulder, 'one of life's more enduring pleasures, I always think.' He removes the toast from the prongs, grunts softly as he rises, and goes to the table to spread it with butter; there's a slice for each of them, each cut neatly in half. The Major settles himself in the one armchair in the room and bids A. bring his plate from the table and sit on his knee. 'Now remember, my child. Not a word to anyone, or they will all come clamouring for buttered toast. Let it be our own little secret.' A. knows he isn't the first boy to have been summoned upstairs by the Major, yet astonishingly it *is* a secret. What takes place in that room belongs to a world which, once left, is instantly erased, so that almost literally there's nothing to tell.

A.'s as partial as any boy to buttered toast, yet it tastes of nothing as he submits to Major Baxendale's urgings: his hand fumbling with A.'s dressing-gown cord, his warm tobacco-y breath in A.'s nostrils, his lips, and his rather prickly moustache, brushing A.'s neck. 'Relax, my child,' he says. 'Relax . . . ' This must be something he needs to say, part of some essential ritual, because in fact A. is neither relaxed nor un-relaxed. He licks the melted butter from his fingers, squirms now and then at the Major's touch, but doesn't feel the least bit frightened or even embarrassed by what's happening. His eyes wander elsewhere: to the fire, the army pictures, a silver-framed photo on the mantlepiece of an unsmiling woman with drawn-back white hair. After the chill temperature in the dorm, the warmth of the Major's room has a cosy almost hypnotic quality. His head droops, his eyelids are heavy.

A. remains half-sitting, half-lying, on the Major's lap, then at last gets up when he's told. He waits while the Major goes across the landing to the lavatory, from which he returns rubbing his hands, behaving now in the same abrupt, no-nonsense manner he uses when teaching. 'Time you were off to bed, I believe.' And more loudly, though there's no one there to hear, without a wink or a sly smile or any other acknowledgment that he's making A. his collaborator in deceit: 'Your maths is coming along very well indeed, my boy. Real progress we're making.' A. makes his way towards the frosted glass door at the end of the landing, then down the single flight of stairs which takes him back into the world of school. When he enters the dormitory, the others are lying in bed reading or talking; none of them speaks to A. as he hangs up his dressing-gown and climbs into bed. Moments later Matron comes in and leads them in reciting the same prayer as on every night before lights out:

Now I lay me down to sleep,
I pray the Lord my soul to keep –

'Now no talking,' Matron says. 'And no tomfoolery, or I'll want to know why.' Then the lights are out, the door closes, and the darkness is total.

*   *   *

A.'s visits to the Major's room last throughout the rest of that term and for a short while into the next. Then, without a word of warning or explanation, he's replaced in the Major's affections by a chubby blond-haired boy called Stamford, who's in the same dormitory as A. Off Stamford goes upstairs every week or two, and A. knows what awaits him there, and perhaps supposes that Stamford knows that he knows, though of course it isn't a question to which he gives any thought. He's now one of those who lie watching as Stamford enters the dorm, watching as he takes off his dressing-gown and slips into bed just before Matron arrives. A.'s miserable for a while, seized by feelings of inadequacy, unworthiness. Wasn't he singled out, chosen above all the other fifty or so boys in the school? Hadn't at least *something* of him been wanted? And now suddenly not-chosen, replaced by a new favourite and back in the ignored anonymous ranks of all the other not-chosens. Not that he recognises any of this; but it's there anyway, and for a time it's the source of an unacknowledged bafflement and pain.

Some months later the boys return to school after the long summer holidays to find that the Major has left. He hasn't said goodbye to any of them and A. will never learn the circumstances of his leaving; whether he was found out and dismissed, or left of his own volition, will be forever a mystery. Perhaps he moved on to some other school, where other mute eleven-year-olds climb the stairs in their dressing-gowns and pyjamas; and then another school, and another, and boys whose names and faces A. has never known and never will know, for whom the Major will become part of their history, whether buried or recalled, and who in the Major's own memories will be indistinguishable as likely as not: simply 'the boy,' object of longings he can neither understand nor resist and can deal with only by blinding himself to their existence.

*　　*　　*

A.'s alone in his flat this warm July evening: an unwanted solitude, an arrangement cancelled at the last moment. In the kitchen he opens a second bottle of white wine, carries it through the spacious high-ceilinged living-room and between the open French windows to a balcony just large enough to accommodate a small wrought-iron table and chair. In the square below him a young man and woman are throwing a Frisbee back and forth, skimming it knee- or waist-high, or tossing it high in the air so it describes a slow graceful arc as it descends. Their voices carry upwards through the still evening air, now bantering, now laughing. A. feels as though he's watching them from another planet rather than a balcony four floors up; they look as though they don't have a care in the world or, if they do have cares, as though they at least know how to cast them aside and have fun once in a while. A mystery really, which A. doesn't care to consider.

He's done well for himself, these last few years. Aged thirty-five, he has a high-up position in the London office of an international investment company, where his fortunes have risen almost more rapidly than he can believe. The last increase they gave him, and the accompanying Christmas bonus, were almost double what he'd expected. There's to be a trip to New York soon, to meet the men at the very top of the company. Hints have been dropped that there could be a place on the board before long.

Most evenings he's out and about somewhere: with people he works with or has met through work; with a girl when, briefly, there is a girl. People enjoy his company; they enjoy the droll cynical remarks he comes out with, his mimicry of mutual acquaintances whose speech patterns and manner-isms he can catch to perfection, making figures of fun of those he's imitating. He's known as a sharp, dangerously witty character. People seem to admire that in him, there are times when they seem to be waiting for him to perform.

When he's alone it's different. Alone he drinks too much and then the cruel wit flees and only the anger behind it is left. When he thinks of his parents, as he invariably does at these times, his rage is almost more than he can contain. To have sent him away like that, just days after his seventh birthday, not even knowing *where* they were sending him, what kind of place it might be or what might happen to him there, not caring enough even to ask themselves these questions – and now, because of his money, his fine new mansion flat off Brompton Road, his exalted place in the world, they expect him to be grateful! The sacrifices they'd made, the things they would have liked but had denied themselves for the sake of their son . . . His mother had said as much, when she and his father had come to see the new flat: 'Well, it just goes to show, dear, how well you can do when you've had a good start in life.' You'd have thought from her tone that it was their achievement as much as his, as though without them he'd never have got to where he was. He'd like to tie his mother to a chair one day and tell her just what that 'good start' had entailed: the bullying, the canings for even the most trifling misdemeanours, the almost constant state of apprehension, of dread that one would unknowingly put a foot wrong and be called to account for it; above all the homesickness, which was surely the worst feeling anyone could know. That absolute loneliness, loss of all one had unwittingly held dear and counted on, loss of hope, loss of one's very soul, or whatever one cared to call it; it was a feeling no one could properly describe. His mother of course would say yes, she knew he'd been homesick to begin with, she'd never forgotten how he'd cried that first time they'd come to see him at school, how terrible his tears had made her feel. But he'd got over it, hadn't he, it hadn't lasted more than a term or two and then he'd been all right. He'd been happy at boarding-school with his friends, it had done wonders for his self-confidence, hadn't it? And what use, in the face of such denial, to tell her that if he'd 'got over' his homesickness it was simply because there'd been no choice but to shut that intolerable feeling out and that in order to do that he'd had to shut out practically every other feeling? She wouldn't understand, any more than his father would; they wouldn't want to understand.

He's succeeded not because of their efforts, but in spite of them. School had been the only true landscape of his life – 'home', in its incongruous indifferent way – and still was, really. The place that should have been home was merely a diversion, an interlude; he knew none of the neighbours' children and didn't know how to get to know them; twice-weekly visits to the pictures brought the only relief from solitude and the sulks. At thirteen, without really trying, he'd won a scholarship to a reputable public school, and then another to Cambridge from where he'd entered the world of finance simply because it held out more than any other the promise of material reward. Still sometimes he wishes he'd refused to do well – had failed his exams, had left school early and become a postman or shop assistant. It would have served them right, such disappointment, would have been the outcome they deserved. But he thanks God he hadn't followed that course. If he had, he'd probably still be living with them in that ghastly cramped little house in the suburbs, too poor to move out. He'd be stuck there with them, for God knows how many years. So he'd succeeded, and now the success seemed hollow, seemed almost like failure, because in their eyes it was their success too.

One day, perhaps, he'd tell them about the Major, let them know just what he'd endured at the hands of that sad old pervert. They'd have no answer to that particular story. His mother would say, Why ever didn't you tell us, dear? and he'd smile pityingly at her, shaking his head. Would you have wanted to know, mother? D'you think I could have believed you'd want to know?

Later that day when he was showing his mother the kitchen – the oak wall-cupboards and worktops, the Mexican floor-tiles, the gleaming new cooker and fridge and washing-machine – she said, 'Well, it's wonderful, dear. And so much space! I hope you make good use of it all.' Her voice changed, taking on a sad almost imploring tone. 'If you just had someone to share it with. I get upset sometimes, thinking of you living all alone.' A. didn't answer. 'You know what I'd like more than anything else in the world, dear?' his mother went on. 'A little grandson or grand-daughter one of these days. One who would come and stay with us sometimes, so we could spoil them and make a fuss of them. It's something I often imagine, you know.' A. turned away; he felt that his whole body was shaking. Then he faced his mother again, controlling his body, shaping his features into an enigmatic smile. 'Well, you never know, mother. These things happen or they don't, we'll just have to wait and see.' She was hurt, he could tell. But not hurt enough, not as hurt as she would have been if he'd said what he wanted to say: *Fat chance.* He wishes he had said it. A wife? A family? Because it's what *you* want? Fat fucking chance. Sorry, mother, I have no plans to waste my time and money on a family, not now, not ever. He was no longer listening while she talked, just looking angrily at his watch and wondering how much longer he'd have to wait until they left.

They'd admired his new flat, and now as he sits on the balcony and drinks his wine he realises that their admiration has ruined it for him. The furniture he's chosen, the rugs, the reproductions of Warhol and Hopper and Buffet on the walls – all of them chosen not because he particularly liked them, but merely to convince himself that he *could* choose, could make the place he lived in an extension of himself, like everyone else did. He could have asked a stranger to furnish the flat, for all it means.

Well, never again, he decides, they've seen his flat for the first and last time. As for visiting them in that terrible little suburban house they still live in, having to listen to their evasions, their platitudes, their recounting of news to which even the word 'trivial' couldn't do justice, well, he won't be doing that again either. They should learn that for them too there's a price to pay; that much at least they should learn, and if it's a painful lesson then perhaps (though it will never happen, of course) they'll ask themselves who's to blame for that pain. Never again. Not until one of them dies and there's a funeral to attend; *then* he'll go, and then he'll leave again, lighter. A. dwells on this thought, seeking to wring some satisfaction from it, but there is no satisfaction. They won't know. They will carry on lying to themselves. Nothing will change, no matter what he might say or do. He thinks of that girl he knew for a time, Anna, who loved him, or claimed to love him, and wanted him to love her back; or at least, she told him, to let her see that on some level he cared. He lived in a cold world and was an unfeeling person, she said when they met for the last time; it was just sad he didn't know it, she said. He laughed, when she'd finished her impassioned little speech, using laughter to disguise a fury he couldn't admit, telling her that if she couldn't bear the world as it was she should do what everyone else did and make up a different one. Take up religion! he said, laughing. Go out and do good deeds! If he'd thought there was the slightest chance of her listening, or if it mattered to him what she thought of him, he'd have told her yes, it was a cold world and you had to be cold to survive in it. People chose not to see it that way, would lie to themselves their whole lives through not to see it, but it was true just the same: face reality or go under, there was no middle way. And then people accuse you of having no heart, because you're prepared to face what they won't face, prepared to see the world for what it is and not let it win. And you can't tell them, can't make them see. There's no way to deal with such people, other than to recognise their self-deceit and forget them; and, above all, not to let them make you waste your precious energies getting mad.

*   *   *

Below him in the fading light the young man and woman have finished their game. The man padlocks the gate behind them and they walk along the pavement towards the far end of the square; the girl has her arm round the man's waist, his hand rests on her bottom in what seems to A. a needlessly boastful proprietorial pose. He watches till they've turned the corner, then pours what's left of the wine into his glass and leans back closing his eyes. He's in a numb, comfortable state. What does it matter after all? The flat. His parents. That Anna woman. What possible bearing do they have on his life? None, when all's said and done. After two bottles of wine, he feels he's rid of them for ever.

A. picks up the empty bottle and glass and carries them into the kitchen, then goes back to lock the French windows. In the bedroom he takes off his trousers and shirt and lies face down on the bed. He closes his eyes and, suspended momentarily in that state that's neither consciousness nor the total lack of it, he sees Major Baxendale's face and is transformed instantly into that small boy climbing the stairs all those years ago; he can smell the toast and the cigarettes, feel the burst of warmth from the gas-fire as he enters the Major's room. He sits on the Major's knee, licks his fingers when he's finished his toast. *Relax, my child* . . . The Major fiddles with his dressing-gown cord and A. lifts his hand and brings it to rest softly on the bristly leathery face. 'It's all right,' he says. 'I understand.' The Major's body tightens. *My child*, he says again and A. hears something in his voice which he recognises as the sound of someone holding back tears. The Major's hands are still, now; A. is still; it's as though they're frozen in that pose, as though they'll be frozen there for ever, freed for the rest of time from the world outside that warm cluttered room. 'I love you,' A. says and the Major's arms reach out and hold him tight. *I know you do, child. I know you do.* The tears run unchecked down the old face; A. wipes them carefully away. 'It's all right,' he says. 'I understand. You're just lonely, that's all.' Hardly have the words died away before, rolling on to his side, A. falls into a drunken sleep. It's unlikely he'll remember this encounter when he wakes. At work these days, among a multiplicity of tasks, he's helping prepare a takeover bid for a firm competitive with his own and is involved in discussions with a large engineering concern whose pension fund his company's hoping to manage. What place for the self and its confusions, amid such pressures?

Them

It's happening again. A Saturday evening and she's in this house she's never set foot in before, a large expensively furnished house belonging to a married couple who have invited her and her husband Michael and three other couples to dinner. She's never met the hosts before, nor does she know any of the guests. Their hosts are people Michael has made friends with, having met the husband through his work as a commissioning editor for a publisher of travel books. Michael likes to make new friends, he loves to 'meet new people,' whom he takes up with all the fervour of someone convinced that *this* friendship will be the deepest and most rewarding of his life. She, on the other hand, does not love meeting new people and would rather be anywhere than here. She imagines herself home this evening, home and safe, curled up on the sofa in front of the television, or engaged in some routine domestic chore, hoovering or ironing. She imagines herself out in a crowd somewhere, alone or with her husband, among people who don't know or notice her. Here in the elegant living-room of this house she sits on a long leather sofa between two heavily-built people, a man and a woman, who might have been placed there for the specific purpose of keeping her where she is. She pictures herself jumping up thrusting them aside, fleeing into the hall and out through the front door into the street, where she will be swallowed by the dark even before her absence is noted and from which she can safely make her way home. But this is not going to happen, so she lifts the bottle of red wine from the long marbled-top coffee-table and refills her glass for the second time in the past few minutes. It should be making her relaxed, the wine, certainly it had been her most fervent hope that it would relax her, but as she'd surely known would be the case, it's no help at all. The terror, the frantic desire to be elsewhere, grow with each second; nor is it helped by her belief that everyone in the room has taken note of how fast she's drinking, thinking things like, Jesus, what's *her* problem? And they'll have noticed too, surely, how it's only her own glass she fills, not even interested or courteous enough to see if anyone else needs a top-up. None of them would realise, for why should they, that the only reason she refrains from offering the bottle is the fear that her shaking hands will give her away. An inadequate person, some kind of emotional cripple, they'll have decided – which of course she is, or she wouldn't be in this state. The person on her left, a balding florid-faced man wearing dark blue jeans and a yellow cashmere sweater, is talking loudly about a rugby match with a man sitting at the other side of the table. England have beaten France apparently, which has made both of them deliriously, boisterously happy, turning those who are sitting closest to

them into little more than an audience for their delight. Her
husband is sitting at the other end of the room, conversing
with a thin, vivid woman who has untidy copper-coloured
hair and is wearing a tight flame-red dress of some faintly
luminous material. This woman, to whom they were intro-
duced when they arrived and whose name, like everyone
else's, she either failed to hear or heard and instantly
forgot, is talking to Michael in an animated confidential
manner, waving her hands, leaning forward to bring their
faces close. Michael nods vigorously, smiling sometimes, as
she talks. He's enjoying himself, though whether this particular woman, this particular conversation, has anything
to do with his enjoyment is open to doubt. Probably not. It's
simply the occasion he enjoys, the sense of being someone
doing the right thing in the right way – convivial, interested,
belonging. Is that unfair, though? she wonders. Patronising?
She tries to think about this, but she's too nervy to concentrate. All the familiar symptoms have gathered: her
mouth dry, stomach tying itself in knots, a persistent
anticipatory buzzing in her ears which seems to come half
from the general hubbub in the room and half from
somewhere deep inside her. She drinks, then puts down her
glass too clumsily and loudly on the table. Her husband
turns quickly at the sound, communicating with his eyes
and with the set of his mouth not one but several messages.
His tightened mouth, and a quick downward glance at her
wineglass, mean: Don't keep drinking like that – you'll be
drunk when everyone else is sober! With his eyes, that one
quick glance apart, he's trying to convey sympathy – 'I
know how you feel.' And reassurance – 'There's nothing to
worry about! Really!' But underlying these messages, and

surely far more deeply felt, are anger and contempt: she's spoiling *his* good time, why can't she just pull herself together and enjoy the evening like everyone else, she's thirty-three years old, for God's sake! And yes she knows all this, and yes she knows how truly pathetic it is, and how natural that it should arouse his contempt. Because he's tried, poor man. For how long now, how many times when an evening like this has been approaching, has he sat listening while she's tried to explain how she feels – tried, at his insistence and without a glimmer of hope on her own part, to 'talk it through'? There's no need for it, he's told her, she has nothing to fear, nothing to be ashamed of, it hurts him to see her so afraid. He's not an intolerant man, but who wants to be married to a child, after all, particularly a child of the sort that used to be labelled 'difficult' or even 'impossible', but now in these enlightened times is usually called 'disturbed'? Last night, sitting with him in the kitchen, she used the phrase 'irrational panic attack', injecting a note of disparaging humour into her voice to show that she could no more take the jargon seriously than he could. But this time he shook his head, his face rigid with what she could interpret only as hatred, and said in the tight, trembling voice of someone pushed beyond endurance: 'Look, if it's *irrational*, then get over it by being *rational*, for Christ's sake! We are supposed to be *rational beings*!' But soon, now, it will be time to eat and she will not be able to eat. The food, if she should manage to swallow even a mouthful, will come back up again and she'll vomit it out over their carefully set festive table. Or worse will happen: the food oozing out of her as liquid evil-smelling shit, uncontroll-able, so that the faces around her freeze in horror and disbelief. This is crazy! she tells herself (as if that would make it end – as if that had ever made it end!), at the same time nodding to the woman next to her who's said something she didn't catch, setting her face in an expression of interest that she's sure is *too* emphatic. Now the woman is asking if Michael is interested in rugby and she smiles as if nothing at all's the matter, as if she's as much at home as everyone else in the room. 'Not as interested as these two apparently are,' she hears herself saying. The woman smiles back at her. 'I'm afraid Jonathan's utterly mad about it,' she says, shaking her head in mock-despair. They are 'making conversation,' and even if she's not making it with any great flair or originality, she's making it adequately, she thinks. But so what? Underneath, she is not remotely similar to these people, is as lost among them as a child who has mistakenly wandered into a room filled with grown-ups. This is all pleasure to them, a casual, comfortable evening. Doubtless they're enjoying the wine, the company, and are looking forward to a meal which, with an enthusiasm which might or might not be sincere, they will pronounce delicious. And then when they're home they'll tell each other their impressions of the evening: whom they liked and didn't like (as if you can tell, from a few hours over a dinner table); what they really thought of the food, the house; whether they were bored or not (and if they were it won't matter, there will still be a pleasing sense of superiority in telling each other so); and who, if any, among those present they might invite to their own next dinner party. In the meantime, mouths open and close, gestures are made, eyes widened or narrowed, and now a great braying laugh is released, causing everyone's heads to turn, everyone wanting to join in the joke. She joins in too, laughing at something she hasn't even heard. But is she laughing too loudly, perhaps? Is she overdoing it, laughing at a joke she hasn't heard in order to prove to the grown-ups that she's as clever as they are? (And naturally the grown-ups would see through this exaggerated display and smile indulgently – if you were a child, that is. Otherwise, as must be happening now, they would just put you down as an uninterestingly sad, nervous person.) But beneath the discomfort of this thought, there's that other, immeasurably worse, discomfort: her bowels on the verge of losing control, it seems, so she sits there clenching herself tight like a child fearful of shaming herself. There's no help from anywhere for what ails her. Certainly she daren't cast even the briefest of glances at her husband, since her terror will be all too evident to him, and his anger to her.

She could plead illness, if she chose. A sudden head-ache, or a quick word in the kitchen with the hostess to explain that her period was due and she was suffering from stomach-cramps. 'I'm really sorry,' she'd say, 'it's such a bore, I was so looking forward to this evening.' It wouldn't be hard to make such an excuse; the hostess would believe her, surely, would sympathise. And then she'd be out of here, almost hysterical with relief. (And perhaps, for people like her, relief, a brief respite from fear, is the closest to happiness they can come?) But it couldn't be done. Her husband would know she'd been lying, but even without his knowing she couldn't do it. It would be 'cheating' and, desperate as she is, she can't allow herself to cheat. Some ingrained and utterly un-self-serving moral sense – or is it just the thought of her husband having to choose between coming home with her or staying on by himself, either of which would spoil his evening? She drinks again, but in that instant between the impulse to drink and the action of picking up and lifting her glass, her hand has decided upon a perverse strategy of its own, has increased its shaking, so all she can do is bring the glass to her mouth as quickly as possible – then push it too hard against her lips so the wine spills down her chin and on to the collar and front of the white blouse she's wearing. 'Oh dear!' the woman sitting next to her exclaims, which is all that's needed to make everyone turn and take notice. She doesn't look at any of them – again, she especially avoids meeting her husband's eyes – but opens her bag and gropes blindly for her hand-kerchief. 'It's all right,' she says, trying to smile, 'it's nothing . . . it's an old blouse, anyway,' she says. Her face is on fire. Everyone is looking at her, seeing not just a woman who's spilled her drink, but a woman who's been drinking too much, who's out of place here, who obviously can't handle something as simple as a dinner party. Pathetic. Pathetic creature. And she must endure this somehow, must smile and shake her head as though in humorous self-reproach, must allow herself to be led across the room and into the kitchen where her hostess, an attractive dark-haired woman, elegant in a grey wool dress and chunky gold necklace, holds a clean tea-towel under a tap and squeezes it out before passing it to her. 'Always happens when you wear white,' this woman says cheerily, 'absolutely guaranteed to happen!' She takes the tea-towel, wipes at the front of her blouse and watches the red stains turn pink. 'It really doesn't matter,' she says, miserably aware of what a nuisance she's being and of the smells of food in the kitchen, the food she'll

be required to eat before long and will not be able to eat, so
that its rich peppery odour causes a dizzying wave of nausea
to rise to her throat. As she hands back the towel, she sees
something in the woman's eyes that suggests sympathy,
concern, and sees herself blurting out everything to her —
'I have this terrible, incomprehensible problem, I cannot
eat among strangers' — and perhaps after all the woman
wouldn't stand in judgement on her but would say something like Oh you poor darling! How awful for you! and
suddenly the fear would be gone and she'd be able to eat
with as much pleasure and conviviality as everyone else.
But it isn't possible to confess how she feels, so she just
smiles and says thank you. 'You're welcome,' the woman
says, smiling back at her. She rinses the towel, then turns
and drapes it over a radiator. 'Actually,' she says, 'you could
borrow a blouse of mine if you like, we're about the same
size, I think. You could bring it back to me next week, or
give it to Michael to give my husband next time they meet.'
'Well – ' she says helplessly. It isn't fair, having to make a
decision at a time like this. She tries to figure it out: Which
would be better, to say yes or no? Which would *sound*
better? but now the woman has taken her hand and is
saying in an intimate, almost conspiratorial tone, as though
the two of them have been friends for years, 'Come along
upstairs, sweet, we'll see what we can find for you.' She
follows the woman through the hall and up the staircase to
the landing. Just as in the living-room, everything's bigger
and cleaner and more elegant than in her own house, a
fragrant vase of flowers on the landing, the lighting sub-
dued, gentle, the white paintwork gleaming — but why all
so strange, so menacing, when all it is, quite harmlessly, is

'someone else's house'? They go through a door into what is obviously the master bedroom and there's suddenly something dreamlike in her situation. For the briefest moment, as the door closes almost soundlessly behind them, she feels just as she does when on the very brink of sleep, as if in fact she's been brought here to sleep: that feeling of relinquishing everything, all challenges and responsibilities abandoned, and even if the dreams awaiting you aren't that nice, at least they'll only be dreams. But it's a fantasy so quickly gone that almost at once it's like something remembered from long ago, like a snatch of music suddenly recalled, giving rise to some lacerating and inexpressible yearning, and all that's left as she watches the woman slide open the door of a wide fitted wardrobe are the symptoms she's been enduring all day: the panic, the churning bowels: the shame. The woman turns to her holding up a blouse that's white like her own but with dark-blue collar and cuffs. 'How about this?' she says, smiling, 'would you like to try it?' She glances at her watch and breathes in sharply. 'My God, the broccoli! It'll be overcooked if I don't get down there!' She rolls her eyes. 'Look, I'll tell you what. You try it on and see if it's okay, and try something else if it isn't – anything you like,' she says and flings out an arm towards the open wardrobe as she leaves. Alone, she sits on the bed trying to will herself to relax, telling herself to breathe slowly, deeply. Faintly from downstairs she can hear music, voices. Them. The grown-ups. She remembers herself as a little girl, alone in her bed: how frightened she was then by her parents' voices downstairs, the slow rise and fall of their voices, then silence, then the voices again; impossible no matter how hard she tried to tell what they were saying. It's a memory that's come to her often recently, making her wonder why she'd been so afraid. Hearing your parents' voices, knowing they were there: wouldn't that be reassuring to most children, make them feel safe in their beds? But it was the not-knowing, she supposed – matters which were beyond her being discussed, things which might have some important bearing on her life, it might even have been her they were talking about, and yet her parents were keeping them hidden from her. 'Life' going on, to which she was not admitted, on which she was unable even to eavesdrop. But this is childish too: trying to substitute for the present a childhood which was entirely uneventful as far as she can recall; no joys, no woes, just a period of her life which lasted a while and then ended. Mostly it's silence she remembers, and solitude: closed doors, long grey afternoons when the rain blurred the view of the garden or the street, and there was nothing she felt like doing. Fear of being alone for ever, fear of being compelled to surrender her solitude and take her place in the world . . .

She removes her stained blouse, letting it fall to the carpet, and puts on the other one. She looks in the full-length mirror, straightens the collar, pulls down the cuffs. Her face when she at last lifts her eyes to it seems, as it almost always does, no different from the face she wore as a child: the same pallor, the same taut, fearful expression, as of someone in permanent readiness for flight. She turns away from the mirror and sits down on the bed. She will have to go downstairs again soon. Downstairs, Michael will be wondering what's keeping her so long, will be angry with her for having made an exhibition of herself. She imagines him fidgeting in his chair, drumming his fingers on its arm, struggling to appear no more concerned about her absence than anyone else. Michael should not have married her. No one should have married her, then there'd be no evenings like this; she'd be alone in her own house or flat somewhere, reading or listening to music; the curtains would be drawn, the world kept out. And Michael would be happy, married to someone who doesn't drag on him as she does. Someone who loves him, as she clearly does not; for, if she did love him, she wouldn't be as she is, love would have changed her, wouldn't it, she would have changed for his sake? She should fall at her husband's feet and beg his forgiveness. It's her fault, it's at her insistence, that she's the person she is. He knows this. Both of them know it.

There are sounds of movement downstairs: chairs scraping, a clatter of shoes on the parquet floor. She gets up and straightens the bedspread, opens the door. If she hurries, she'll be able to sit down at the same time as everyone else, instead of drawing attention to herself by arriving when they're already seated. She has to hurry, even though her mouth's dry as ashes, her bowels turning to water. There's an irony there and she tries brokenly to laugh at it as she reaches the stairs.

Encounters

In the evening sometimes – often enough, these days, that it seems to Richard like every evening – his wife Alex tells him who she's seen or spoken to on the phone that day and what's going on in their lives. Jo's upset because her father has to go into hospital next week. Rebecca and James are taking their son out to dinner, to celebrate his A-Level results. Sandra's in a good mood because she and Duncan are off on holiday to Crete on Saturday. Richard grunts occasionally, or nods; now and then he remembers to try to arrange his features into the expression of someone who's listening, interested. It is without meaning somehow, the words themselves seem to have no meaning, *upset, happy, celebrating,* even though he must have spoken them thousands of times himself before now without once stopping to question their use. But now as he hears them from Alex's lips there is a mystery to them. What can it matter that someone's being taken into hospital, or has passed a few exams, or is off abroad for a fortnight? How is anything changed? How is the *scenario* changed? He feels he's choking on these thoughts; there's the sensation of something caught in his chest, impossible to expel. He pictures Alex listening earnestly throughout the day, smiling, frowning, pursing her lips, widening her eyes, committing everything to memory so she can repeat it to him. But why? Is it her way of telling him she has a life independent of her life with him, her own friends, her own preoccupations? If it is, then perhaps he should tell her that he knows that by now, that he has his own life too, only unlike her he doesn't see any point in boring anyone else with its dreary details. He recalls a sentence in a novel he once read: 'The more useless I realise it is to talk the more I need to talk.' He'd like to show Alex this sentence, but he's forgotten the title of the novel. Anyway, Alex would be insulted if he repeated it to her. She'd feel patronised, would accuse him of being 'chauvinistic' or 'negative' or probably both.

'Poor Jo's been having such a hard time recently,' Alex says, and although he sighs and shakes his head as if in commiseration, he's thinking, So what other kind of time is there, for Christ's sake! – angry because he can't express this thought to anyone but himself and because Alex talks on and on without showing the slightest awareness of how he feels or, if she is aware, just steaming on regardless. She wants to change him, he decides; she wants to turn him into herself, make him as involved as she is with all these lives, because that's how people should be, in her eyes. That's what behind it all, he thinks, even if she doesn't know it.

*   *   *

'Cheers,' he says, lifting his glass. It's the lunch-hour and he and his colleague Fred Addenbrooke are sitting at a corner table in their usual pub, having their usual meal of a pint

and a sandwich. Eight or nine years they've worked together; they've met each other's wives, visited each other's
homes, worked late and gone out and got drunk together,
though none of these things for some time now. Fred's
probably the closest he's had to a friend, these past few
years. Not that Richard would dream of using that word;
but Fred, he thinks, who's so anxious for friendship, would
use it only too eagerly. Recently Richard's found himself
wondering if Fred really knows anything about him after all
this time, or believes he knows anything – anything, that is,
that would enable him to regard what's just a limited and
undemanding compatibility as something deeper and more
valuable. And so what if he does? If he wanted to, Richard
could make a conscious effort to deepen their relationship,
maybe talk about himself a bit more, to let Fred know he
trusts and values him, or maybe question Fred about his
own life. But what would be the point of such a deliberate
move, when he doesn't actually need a close friend, or care
about Fred's life, or care that Fred knows so little of his?

But that's it with Fred, he thinks. Needing approval all
the time, needing to prove he has all the things people are
meant to have, if their lives are to be considered worth-
while. I have a wife and children! I have a home! I have a
job! I have a good friend! As if, seen to possess these things,
he should be entitled to some sort of certificate of validity
which will enable him to mingle with others on equal terms.

Like a puppy, Richard thinks. Licking your hand and
waiting to be patted. It surprises him that he's failed to see
this before in Fred, when suddenly it's so blindingly obvious.

The publishing company they work for is on the verge of
being taken over by a far larger concern, an American

'multimedia' corporation which opened an office in London two or three years ago and has already snapped up several businesses like their own: small to medium-size companies which had been struggling to break even each year and lacked the resources to do anything but hang on and hope. And then the Americans move in and take the pieces they want and discard the rest. Or, if not the Americans, some other large company looking to see what it can lay hands on for next to nothing. In the past eighteen months, seven people out of twenty-five in Richard's company have been laid off. Take away a few of those who are left, slash the rest of the overheads, and you're looking at profit.

Fred shakes his head, his thin face even more mournful than usual. Like Richard, he's in his mid-forties; but he has a larger and more expensive house than Richard, has three children to Richard's one. Sombre, he chews the last of his sandwich, then picks up his paper napkin and wipes his lips. 'It's not a question of whether *anyone* goes, it's a question of who does and who doesn't . . . If anyone,' he adds hollowly. 'You'll be okay, probably. So will Martin and Ray, and Diane too, I shouldn't wonder. But for the rest of us' – he throws up his arms, in what seems to Richard an unnecessarily dramatic gesture – 'who on earth can say what might happen?' Richard doesn't answer. He turns and gazes through the window into the street. It's begun raining since they entered the pub, a sudden quite heavy summer shower. The sun's still shining, the puddles glisten on the pavement and in the street. People are hurrying for shelter or already standing in doorways and under shop awnings. The words of a song come into his head: . . . *it isn't raining rain, you know, it's raining . . . vi-o-lets!* and keep running through it all the time Fred's

talking in his low, earnest voice about the takeover, the
threat to jobs, the terrible uncertainty of it all. Richard feels
not the slightest need to try to forget the song and listen to
what Fred's saying. The thought that this is all so important
to Fred, and that Fred hasn't the faintest idea that his words
are being drowned by the banal words of a song, has a
satisfying absurdity to it. It bothers him, though, that Fred
won't know this; and it bothers him that the song, having
taken root in his head, will probably stay there long after
he's wished it gone.

'You just can't tell with these bastards,' Fred's saying.
He's working himself up, his voice shaking slightly, rage
and impotence in his eyes. 'Asset strippers. They'd kill their
own bloody grandmothers, if they could make a few bucks
on it.'

He stops, finally, but there's still that dark, glowering
look on his face. He's breathing heavily, exhausted by his
mood. Richard shrugs.

'Well,' he says slowly, 'I guess they'll do whatever
they think needs doing. Anyway, what's the alternative? To
struggle on as we are? How long d'you think that would last?'
He has nothing to say about the impending takeover. Several
times he's thought to himself *What happens, happens* and
when in his own or someone else's office he's been forced to
listen to people's views on the subject, their speculations,
their fears, he's done so without ever feeling involved. Why
do people need to talk about it so much? Do they think that
by talking about it they can stop it happening, or make it
happen in some way which will hurt others but not them?
Now and again he acknowledges they're right to worry: most
of them, like him, have families to think of, mortgages, bills

to be met. But even while seeing it, he can't worry himself. There are times, in fact, when what would ordinarily be perceived as disaster, the takeover accomplished, his job gone, takes on a triumphant aspect. Everything blown to pieces: it would be right, somehow, there would be a kind of justice there, if he were to go home to his wife and son one evening to tell them that all the things that meant so much to them – and that they had taken so much for granted all this time! – were to be lost to them for good. Alex could give up her part-time job and look for something full-time; Oliver could sacrifice his allowance; and, most drastic of all, they'd almost certainly have to sell the house and move into something smaller. He imagines Alex's rage, her tears, when he breaks the news to her, how grudgingly she'll accept that there was nothing he could have done. *You see?* he'll be thinking. *You see, now?*

Nothing ever goes any further in this recurring fantasy. No redundancy money, no possibility of finding work elsewhere; just a *fait accompli*, to which his wife and son will have no choice but to submit.

'Same again?' he asks, pointing at Fred's empty glass; and although he'd normally be far too much in thrall to his superiors to extend his lunchbreak beyond the allotted one hour, Fred says, 'Why not?' in the defiant tone of someone who's had just about enough of being pushed around and isn't going to stand for it any longer. Richard gets up and carries their glasses to the bar. He imagines Fred telling his wife about it later: *Sod it, I thought, why should I work for them like a slave, when they can't even tell me what's going on?* This is it, he thinks, returning to the table with their drinks, Fred Addenbrooke's grand gesture.

Fred drinks hurriedly, clearly regretting having allowed Richard to buy another round; some of the beer trickles down his chin and on to his shirt-collar. 'Listen,' he says cautiously, 'I don't want to step out of line or anything, or ask you to say anything against your will – but you haven't heard something I haven't, have you? You haven't been told anything?'

Richard takes his time drinking. He gives Fred a surprised, enquiring look. 'Anything about what?'

Fred looks baffled for a moment. 'The takeover. I just wondered if you'd heard – if you knew something – '

'Not a thing. Why?'

'You seem so calm,' Fred says. 'You act like it doesn't bother you, somehow. As if you already know you're all right.' Richard sees sweat on Fred's upper lip, his eyes moving quickly, nervously; he looks during these moments like someone on the verge of breakdown. 'No, listen, I'm sorry,' Fred says. 'Forget I asked you that question. I shouldn't have asked it. I'm sorry.'

'I don't know any more than you do,' Richard says. 'Even less, maybe.' That ridiculous song sounds in his head, so that he's barely conscious of what he's saying. *So keep on looking for that bluebird . . . and listening for his song!* 'Well, I must say,' Fred says, 'you're certainly taking it amazingly calmly.' He gazes disconsolately into his glass. 'I only wish I could be as relaxed as you are.'

'Tell yourself there's nothing you can do,' Richard says. 'Ask yourself, what's the use of worrying?' Knowing, of course, that Fred's about the last person in the world who could take such advice and enjoying, as far he enjoys anything, the thought that Fred will envy him hugely, will despise himself for worrying so much, for being unable to change himself into someone who doesn't worry, who can keep his head like his friend Richard can.

Richard swallows the last of his beer, then gets up and lifts his jacket from the back of his chair. 'We're pawns in this game. You and me both. There's nothing we *can* do but wait and see.' Fred puts on his own jacket. The look on his face is the look of someone striving to be other than what he is, unable to ask himself whether what he is might not be as inadequate as he believes, might simply be human. As they make their way to the door, Richard claps an arm round his shoulders. 'Back to the grindstone, then,' he says, 'for as long as it lasts.'

*   *   *

There's no answer when he knocks on his son's door, but he opens it and goes in anyway. Oliver, who is fourteen, is lying on the bed with his headphones on. (God knows what he's listening to; all Richard can get from it is a series of metronomic thuds.) The bed's unmade, the duvet twisted beneath him, the pillow propped between his head and the headboard. The room's a mess: rumpled clothes on the carpet, cassettes and CD's scattered about. The walls are covered with posters for pop concerts and 'all-nite raves'. The air is thick with body smells.

Oliver removes his headphones and puts them down beside him on the bed. 'Hi,' he says dully and leans forward letting the pillow slide down behind him so he can lie flat. Richard thinks for a moment of asking him if he's ever thought about hanging up his clothes in the wardrobe sometimes, or opening a window, but it doesn't seem worth it.

His son's probably as incapable of changing his habits as he is of changing his looks: he's a fat, lumpy boy, *utterly grace-less*, as Richard said once to Alex, who seems to ask nothing of life except that it should make no unreasonable demands of him, which, as far as Richard can tell, means no demands at all. Richard thinks about his son as little as possible: this boy he has helped bring into the world, who is supposed to be a part of him in some way and with whom he lives now in a state which veers between indifference and hostility, depending on the extent to which either of them is intruding upon, which is to say crossing the path of, the other. He remembers once in a while how he wept at Oliver's birth and how during the first few months of Oliver's life he sometimes woke up terrified in the night convinced his son had died, then tiptoed across the landing to Oliver's room and put his ear to his face to hear him breathing. Now it seems like some sort of game he remembers. All those delights and anxieties they experienced, that absolute pre-occupation with Oliver, and with their own responses to him, were a kind of childishness in themselves, as if their son was a unique and engrossing new toy they'd been given. How could they have known then that their entrancing new baby would grow into this sour, resentful creature who, if he has any redeeming features, seems bent on disguising them? They couldn't have known, but Richard can't help feeling they should have.

'He is not "utterly graceless",' Alex said. 'He's just a teenager.' As if nothing was more sure to her than that eventually Oliver would shed his present self like an old skin, change into someone they could tolerate and even enjoy once in a while. Richard wonders if she believes this;

he certainly doesn't. There aren't any grounds for believing it. Far more likely, almost certain in fact, is that Oliver will remain exactly what he is, just another addition to the countless number of helpless and unattractive people in the world, people who don't know why they're so helpless and have no other destiny than to endure the knowledge that they are. One might resist these thoughts, even fight to prevent their coming true, but against what odds? One might think it all one's own fault, for not having been the parent one might have been, but then whose fault would that be? It isn't a question of fault. Just life, somehow. Often nowadays when he sees a pregnant woman on the street, or someone carrying a baby or pushing a pram, he wants to seize them by the arm and make them see what he sees. Why so happy? he wants to ask them. Why so *sure*? Then it occurs to him that someone might have looked at him fourteen years ago in just the same way, someone who knew the world then as he knows it now. Such continuing folly, the cycle continued generation upon generation: how could one not be incredulous?

Now Alex has found money missing from her purse again, for the third time in only two or three months. A five-pound note the first time, then a ten-pound note, and the day before yesterday a fiver again. It has to be Oliver who took them; no one else could have done, Alex said. She's spoken to Oliver about it and he's denied all knowledge of the thefts, so now she's asked Richard to speak to him, as if he might succeed where she's failed. When Richard suggested that it wasn't quite as terrible as she thought, that all children steal because if they see something they want they see it as their right to have it, or because they have this compulsion to live dangerously, to push things to the edge now and again, she said angrily, 'All children are not like that, Richard. Not even most of them. I want you to talk to him this evening,' she said, and here he is removing a pile of clothes from the chair in front of Oliver's computer before sitting down. He's as unhappy as Oliver is that he's here, exhausted before the conversation's begun. For a moment or two he gazes through the window at the pale sky, as if it holds out the possibility of flight. Then he forces himself to look at Oliver and, trying to sound concerned, trying at least not to sound as averse to the whole matter as he feels, says, 'Listen, your mother's told me about this money that's gone missing from her purse. Three times, she says. She says you've been stealing from her. Is that right? Have you?'

Oliver's face reddens slightly. He frowns, clasping his hands behind his head and gazing down at his feet.

'I don't know anything about it,' he says peevishly. 'I've told her. I haven't got a clue what she's talking about.'

'So where did it go, then?' Richard says. 'Perhaps you can think of something we haven't.' Already it's clear to him that Oliver isn't going to confess. Immediately below them, in the kitchen, Alex is washing up the supper things. She's sent him up here for nothing. He and Oliver know it, and she doesn't; in this, if in nothing else, he feels at one with his son.

'I don't know any more than you do,' Oliver says. He pauses, picking a loose thread from the sheet and rubbing it between his finger and thumb. 'Maybe it wasn't even there in the first place. Maybe she spent it on something herself.'

'I don't think so. She knows how much money she had. Mum always knows how much money she's got in her purse.'

Oliver raises his eyebrows, as though to say, Maybe she does maybe she doesn't; how would I know? and Richard wonders briefly if for once Alex hadn't known how much money she had, if she'd broken into a note and forgotten about it, or just miscounted. She's always been a capable and well-organised person, but people do sometimes change, especially if they're not as contented as they used to be. And Alex isn't contented; even though she's never actually admitted it, the signs have been there for quite some time now, and unmistakeable: sudden irrational outbursts of anger, a tendency to react to small domestic mishaps as if they were major disasters, and sometimes when she doesn't know he's watching her a look of barely controlled tension on her face – something in the set of the mouth, the jaw-line – as if she's holding in check some inexpressible rage. So perhaps she's been losing control a little. Perhaps, and not unreasonably, she feels cheated by life and is looking for someone to blame. Richard imagines himself going downstairs and confronting her with this idea; he imagines her confessing, apologising. But it won't happen, of course. He doesn't believe for a moment she's lost track of her money. He just wants to believe it, so this whole laborious matter can be closed.

'Listen,' he hears himself saying, 'if you've got into some sort of trouble over money, if you owe money to someone at school or something, you should come to us and tell us. These things can be dealt with usually. Only we have to know, we can't help if you won't tell us.' He looks straight into Oliver's eyes as he says this, partly to impress upon Oliver the absolute sincerity of the words and partly in the hope that by will-power alone he can coerce Oliver into admitting that yes, he was in trouble, he needed the money, he should have asked instead of taking. He needs to hear this from his son, he's pleading with Oliver to understand and accommodate him in this – just this once! – even if he didn't steal the money. Just do this for me! Own up, please, and I'll never ask you for anything again!

Oliver raises his head slightly and for once looks directly back at his father. There are no signs of embarrassment or guilt on his face, just a theatrical expression of annoyance and fatigue. 'I am not in any trouble,' he says. 'I do not owe any money to anyone. I did not take any money from Mum's purse.'

'Okay,' Richard says. 'All right, then. You say you didn't and Mum says you did. What am I supposed to think?'

'Whatever you like, I suppose,' Oliver says in a lofty, patronising tone. And why not? Have either of his parents even a shred of evidence that he stole the money? Does he need any strategy but simple denial? Clearly he doesn't; and perhaps beyond this knowledge there's the recognition that his father's really quite easy to deal with, certainly a lot easier than his mother who's gone on and on at him as if trying to make him confess through sheer exhaustion. His father is more collaborator than accuser. He doesn't want the truth, all he wants is to be rid of the obligation to try to establish the truth, so he can go back downstairs and read the newspaper or something. Nothing can happen. There will be a period of awkwardness and bad feeling in the house, endurable because he'll know that sooner or later something new will happen which will bring it to an end, or the subject will just naturally wear itself out. All this will be known to him, Richard thinks, without his knowing he knows it. But he's safe; that much he does know.

Oliver stares up at the ceiling. Richard sits clasping and unclasping his hands between his thighs. He looks at one of Oliver's posters, Ab-so-lutely The Rave All-Niter Of The Year! Three Super-Star DJs! and wonders if he should try showing an interest in Oliver's life, maybe ask him about these superstars whose names mean nothing to him; though at the same time he's forced to recognise that any show of interest would be fake, and that Oliver would know this, and that the conversation, should it ever happen, would be an ordeal for them both.

'Okay,' he says, 'We'll forget about it for now. We'll leave it open. But if money goes missing again from Mum's purse, not just tomorrow or the day after, but any time, we'll assume it *was* you who took it and it'll be deducted from your allowance. Do you understand?' 'Yes,' Oliver says, without looking at him. 'I understand,' he says, his voice dismissive, arrogant, now that he knows he's off the hook. Richard doesn't mind this; he's getting out now and would tolerate just about anything from his son. But he still has the feeling that something more needs saying, that Alex will expect something more, and when he's opened the door he turns and gives Oliver a long, serious look.

'One more thing. If you are in trouble of any kind, you should come and talk to us about it. Problems don't get solved on their own, as a rule.'

'I know,' Oliver says. 'I would talk to you, if there was a problem.'

'Fine. I'm glad to hear it.' Richard manages to smile faintly. 'Well, I guess that's it, then,' he says. 'You can get back to your music.'

Oliver doesn't answer. He's already picking up his headphones as Richard closes the door. Richard stands on the landing thinking he hasn't done badly after all. There's been no admission of guilt from Oliver, but at least he'll be able to tell Alex that he's warned him what will happen next time, if there is a next time, and that Oliver doesn't seem to be in any trouble they should know about. He can come out of it sounding pretty good, if he finds the right way to tell it. It would be even better if Oliver had confessed, of course, but then Alex hadn't been able to get him to do that either, so how can she blame him for having failed?

*   *   *

The film he's watching is straight off the TV movie conveyor-belt. A city somewhere in America; a lone policeman, out to nail the mob; fights, car chases, the policeman's wife and son threatened, corrupt superiors in the force issuing veiled threats to lay off. Richard lies on the sofa, sipping from a can of beer, and Alex sits in an armchair reading, stopping now and then to give the television a sour incredulous look. Although she'll watch a documentary once in a while, or a film or play that's had good reviews, she disapproves strongly of television. 'Just watching for the sake of watching – I don't know how you can do it night after night.' Richard replies to these accusations not because he feels the need to defend himself, but because Alex says things in a manner that demands a response and because it gives him the chance to make one or two quite dark observations that he might not otherwise be able to make. He's tired these days, he might say, the pressures at work are getting to him, he seems to be running out of energy, somehow; nothing seems worth doing, somehow. Once he said that it was perhaps just part of the ageing process and Alex said sharply, 'You're forty-seven, Richard. You're hardly Methuselah, for heaven's sake!' Even if he wanted to, it would be hard to explain to Alex that he watches television not because he's interested in what's on, but because he can't think of anything better to do. Sometimes he dozes off for half an hour, then wakes and lies on the sofa switching back and forth between the five channels. Thoughts that have no connection with what he's watching pass through his head, but it's the television that prevents them lingering. And this is its point, he thinks, this is what people mean, isn't it, when they talk about 'unwinding in front of the box'?

Now as usually happens around half-past ten or eleven, Alex closes her book and gets up. 'I think I'll go on reading in bed,' she says. She comes over to the sofa and Richard reads the book's title, *Lives Of Girls And Women*. It would be a good book, a 'serious' book, Alex would read nothing else, and he wonders what point there is to all this seriousness if at the end of it all one's life adds up to nothing more than a succession of inconsequential news items. Alex smiles at him, leaning down and taking his hand. 'Okay?' she says, looking into his eyes. 'Sure,' he says, 'I'll be up myself before long.'

Alex doesn't let go of his hand. Her grip on it tightens, as if she's trying to pass some message to him through their joined fingers, as if she's pleading with him to respond. This is what he believes, at any rate, and he feels threatened by it, almost panic-stricken. He looks up at her and smiles, says, 'I'll just stay till the end of this film, dear. Then I'll be up.' He increases the pressure of his own fingers, hoping she'll read into the gesture whatever it is she wishes to read and won't ask anything more of him right now. And it works apparently, or if it doesn't Alex must have decided to pretend that it does, because she lets go of him and moves towards the door. 'See you in a bit, then,' she says. 'Half an hour or so,' he says, 'forty minutes max.' Then she's gone and for a minute or more he lies on the sofa with his eyes closed. He's exhausted suddenly, a great yearning for sleep, for oblivion, has come over him, but it's too early yet to follow Alex upstairs so he gets up and goes into the kitchen and takes another can of beer from the fridge. The movie goes on. By now the hero has found a member of the mob who, in return for his own safety, will tell everything he knows. The rest of the film will reveal whether or not the bad guys – including the corrupt police officials, one of whom is actually guarding the stool-pigeon with the hero – will 'get to him' before the trial. Nothing unexpected will happen, there will be not a single line of dialogue that isn't a cliché. There's something comforting in such cynically conceived staleness; he has the feeling of being secretly in cahoots with the film's makers, endorsing their cynicism. It's the sort of job he should have himself, he thinks: no bother at all, and if anyone accuses you of peddling rubbish you simply refer them to the viewing figures.

He watches the film to its end, switches to a channel on which four people are discussing an art exhibition that's just opened. When he's drunk the last of his beer, he gets up and turns the set off. By now, with any luck, Alex will have given up waiting for him and fallen asleep. There's no sound from Oliver's room, so probably he's asleep too. He carries the ashtray and empty beer can into the kitchen, throws the can and empties the ashtray into the bin, closes the kitchen window and goes back along the passageway to bolt the front door. In the bedroom he finds Alex lying on her back open-mouthed, snoring faintly. He picks up the book from her duvet, puts it on the bedside table and switches off her lamp. Then there's the ritual of changing into his pyjamas, going into the bathroom to pee and clean his teeth, turning the landing light off, coming back into the bedroom and winding the alarm-clock. He resents having to perform these same mundane tasks every night, resents having no choice but to perform them, and when at last he's in bed and reaching out to switch off his own lamp, he feels he's survived an ordeal. The day's over, finally. Six hours of sleep await him, six hours of having neither to act nor react, of being left alone. These last few moments before sleeping, lying on his side with his back towards Alex, his head finding just the right angle, just the right resting-place on the pillow, are the best of his day.

Now, though, when sleep is surely only seconds away, Alex murmurs his name. Her hand slides under his pyjama-jacket and comes to rest on the small of his back. He doesn't move. He holds his breath, praying she hasn't woken herself with the gesture.

'You're so tense,' Alex says sleepily. Her hand moves on his back. 'You should relax,' she says. 'You mustn't be tense like this. It's not good for you.' He doesn't answer. Another few seconds, he tells himself, and she'll have fallen asleep again or will assume he has. But, 'It isn't good for you,' she repeats. 'You shouldn't. You shouldn't be so tense all the time. You think I don't notice . . . ' Her hand moves again, feeling its way to his ribs. He understands that she's touching him because she needs to touch him – needs to be touched in

return, needs to be spoken to, at least! – but there's nothing
he can do. He wants none of these things. Co-existence
without demands is what he wants, a mutual leaving alone
of one another. If she really wanted to relieve the tension
she senses in him, she'd remove her hand and turn away
and sleep. He imagines saying this to her, 'Just let me sleep,
for Christ's sake!' and it's not so much the knowledge that it
would be cruel that keeps him from saying it as the reali-
sation that he would have to live for weeks or even months
afterwards with the consequences: the hurt, the anger. And
how could he blame her for being angry? Why should it be
so hard, after all, why should anything be easier than for a
husband to put his arm round his wife, at night, in their bed,
and offer her whatever comfort he can, even if that comfort
resides nowhere but in the fact of his recognising she needs
it? He sees all this, yet he can't act on it, or even regret that
he can't. The desire to be left alone is so overpowering that
there's simply no room for anything else. But Alex clearly
isn't going to fall asleep again in a hurry, so he places his
hand over hers and says, 'I'm really not that tense, all things
considered.' 'What d'you mean?' she says, suddenly alert.
'All what things?' 'Work and everything. The takeover.' 'But
I thought you said you'd be all right. I thought we didn't
need to worry about it.' 'We don't probably. It's just that I
can't be a hundred percent sure.' 'But you said we were
safe, didn't you? I thought you said there was nothing to
worry about.' 'Well, I didn't think there was. You can't
always tell with these things.'

Alex says softly, 'Christ,' and the two of them lie there in
silence for a time. Then, 'Tell me,' she says. 'Should I worry
or not? What's going on, exactly?' 'I don't know. I wish I did

know.' 'So we could lose everything, then. Is that what you're saying?' 'I don't know.'

Alex removes her hand and turns abruptly away from him. The anger comes off her like heat, like an odour. 'Christ almighty,' she says. Richard lies on his back, his eyes closed. For the very briefest of moments, it occurs to him that he could easily move close to her again, could tell her there's really no need to worry because even if he does lose his job they'll still each have other and will be able to find some way out. Who knows? he could say, it might turn out to be all for the best. But he doesn't feel like it. Of course it would be better for Alex and he'd be able to tell himself afterwards that he'd done what he could, had put her first and himself second. *We are not suited*, he thinks; the words have a pleasing finality to them, and almost at once he yawns and stretches and turns on his side. Alex has fallen asleep already, from the sound of her breathing. Panikova.

*   *   *

His Uncle Ronald's bed is one of three in a room on the second and top floor of the hospice. The other two beds, which Richard has to pass in order to reach him, are occupied by old men too. They lie on their backs silent and unmoving, as though in joint rehearsal for death; neither of them stirs as he goes by. The room is hot, airless, filled with a sweetish medicinal odour. Above his uncle's bed there's a crude painting of a sailing-boat, blue sea, blue sky, a shore-line of palm-trees and sand.

His uncle is lying on his side, a single white sheet covering him. His eyes are closed, but now as Richard reaches the bed they open as abruptly as if at the pressing of a switch.

They stay fixed on his nephew, blank as a doll's glass eyes. 'Richard,' he says, without expression. He seems to be naked under the sheet. A naked foot and ankle and calf are exposed and one naked arm dangles over the edge of the bed, fingers almost touching the grey lino. Richard notices three or four thin transparent tubes disappearing under the sheet, but doesn't stop to consider what their functions or destinations might be. They're to do with dying, what else is there to know?

'That's right, Uncle Ronald,' he says, 'it's your nephew Richard come to see you.' He can't remember how long it's been since he last saw his uncle. Earlier in their marriage, he and Alex had invited him for the day every two or three months; it had been an easy gesture to make, rewarding to let him see how happy they were in their bright new life. His own marriage, which by all accounts had not been happy, had ended several years before theirs had begun, when his wife had died of breast cancer. It had been a childless marriage, and when he came to see them his uncle talked incessantly about the only two things in his life which seemed to mean anything to him: the war, in which he'd served in both the North African and Italian campaigns, though never rising above the rank of corporal, and his job with a security company where, to hear *him* tell it, he was never given a position commensurate with his worth but had been passed over time and again in favour of people younger and less able than he – people whose faces fit, people who 'knew who to suck up to,' he said venomously. He was an embittered and monotonous old man, and they stopped inviting him eventually. 'We should ask Uncle Ronald over,' one of them would say, but that was as far as it ever went. They'd had enough of him; and, besides, they were experiencing the first tremors of their own dissatisfactions by then, were becoming too resentful and inward-looking to enjoy playing host. Richard knew as well as Alex did that they ought to invite him, that there was really no excuse for just cutting him out of their lives, but he never got round to it. He'd surrendered enough of himself, one way and another. Why should he turn over practically an entire Saturday to some sad old fart who'd do nothing but bore him to breaking-point?

And now the old fart's dying. The young man who'd opened the front door to Richard a few minutes ago had told him there was no questioning this, no possibility of recovery. 'All we can do is make his last few days as peaceful and pain-free as we can,' he said, and Richard said, 'Well, that's good of you. Thank you for that,' in a tone which he hoped sounded sincere. The young man waited a moment, then said, 'Listen, if you need me, I'm here. Okay?' and went back into his office. It wasn't exactly an abrupt departure, but as he climbed the stairs Richard felt for a moment that the young man had seen him more clearly than he wished to be seen.

Now he pulls up a chair and sits down, leans forward and touches his uncle's arm. 'Well, they seem to be doing everything they can for you, Uncle Ronald,' he says. 'They seem like really good people here.' 'They are,' his uncle says. His voice is slurred, distant, like that of a child on the edge of sleep. 'They're won'ful. Won'ful people.' 'Well, that's nice,' Richard says. 'That's good. I'm glad to hear it.' Already he's thinking almost frantically about getting away from his uncle and out of this place. He could drive into town, have a drink or two somewhere before driving home. Somewhere quiet, somewhere where no one will know him, just as soon as he decently can.

'Are you comfortable?' he asks. 'Is there anything you need? Anything I can get you?'

His uncle's eyes fill with tears suddenly. The tears run down his face and, relieved at having something to do other than smile and hunt laboriously for words, Richard takes out his handkerchief and wipes them away. Then, speaking almost as clearly as if he was perfectly well, but in the inflexionless tone of someone making an announcement of absolutely no importance, his uncle says: 'It hasn't been much of a life.'

The words hang in the air between them. 'What d'you mean?' Richard says. 'What d'you mean, "Not much of a life"?'

'Done nothing with it. Didn't have much of a job, didn't have any children. Wouldn't even call it a life. Call it a wasted life.'

'But that's absurd,' Richard says. He laughs, to show his uncle just how absurd he finds it. 'I mean, what about the war? All those years of active service you saw? Isn't that something to look back on and be proud of?'

His uncle looks at him blankly, as if baffled by the question. He makes a sound something like a laugh, bringing a froth of tiny bubbles to his lips.

'Didn't have any choice. Got called up and went. Couldn't get out of it.' Richard tries to think of an answer to this, but can't. He would have said the same thing himself probably, in his uncle's place.

'But, Uncle,' he says, 'it's like that for everyone, by and

large. How many of us can be Shakespeare, or Winston Churchill, for goodness' sake? We just get by, most of us. We do the best we can. That's what life's about, most of the time.'

'Not your life,' his uncle says. 'You got a good life. Lovely wife and son to look after. Good job. Lovely home. How can you say your life's wasted? You can't. You can't say it.' He belches suddenly, the sound like an explosion in the small room. 'Not like my life,' he says, and Richard feels that same choking sensation he gets so often these days, something raw and hot and barely containable rising from the pit of his stomach: *Your* life? *Your* lousy deal? But it passes almost at once. It's a joke, isn't it? His, of all families. The only family his uncle knows and he's made of their lives everything he failed to make of his own. It is a joke. He imagines telling Alex about it when he gets home. Not that Alex will think it amusing, but at least there'll be some fleeting satisfaction in showing her that he does. But this does nothing to curb his desire to get out of here or, at the very least, to devise some programme for escape that will establish a limit to how long he has to stay.

He watches the tears fall, thinking how strange it is that they make no sound and that his uncle shows no sign of being aware of them. No changes of facial expression, even; just the tears falling, as if someone's turned on a tap. 'You're a good boy, Richard . . . ' His uncle's eyes are closed, his voice distant again. 'A good boy . . . only one come 'n' see me . . . di'n't forget your old uncle . . . '

Then, abruptly, he's asleep, lips parted, face incongruously childlike in repose. Behind Richard, one of the old men sighs softly, shifts in his bed and mumbles something inaudible. Sweat breaks out under Richard's arms. He gets up and takes off his sweater and hangs it over the back of his chair. Five hours driving, from London to here and back, and for less than ten minutes. Perhaps his uncle's said the only thing he needed to say, the one thing he'd been saving for his nephew's arrival. Perhaps this is all he's driven here for.

It's a no-win situation, he thinks. If he leaves, his uncle might wake and feel abandoned. If he doesn't, his uncle might sleep for hours. There's no telling how long he might have to sit here.

The door opens and the same young man who let him in enters the room. 'Ah, he's asleep, is he?' he says, peering down from the end of the bed. He has an earnest, boyish face, pale blue eyes, thinning red hair combed carefully across his scalp. 'He'll sleep for some time, probably. Hours, maybe. You might just as well leave, to be honest.'

Richard hesitates. 'You think so?'

'He could be asleep for hours. You're lucky he was awake when you got here.' The young man looks at his watch. 'You can stay if you want to, of course. But I wouldn't advise it. Not with that drive back to London ahead of you.

Richard doesn't move. He's out of here now, he can afford a show of reluctance.

'If he does wake up, I'll tell him it was at my suggestion you left.' The young man smiles at him. 'How's that?' he says, smiling.

'Well . . . okay, then,' Richard says. 'Thank you.' He gets up and picks up his sweater and pulls it over his head. *Done*, he thinks. *Over*. The young man moves ahead and opens the door. "Actually I've got something for you,' he says, following Richard along the narrow landing and down the stairs. 'It's here in the office. Something your uncle wants you to have.'

'Oh, right,' Richard says vaguely. He doesn't wonder for more than a moment what it might be. Some minor keepsake probably, something of 'sentimental value'.

The office is a dusty cluttered little room, furnished on the cheap: two desks covered with files and papers and crowded stacks of trays; a draining-board with mugs and teaspoons and an electric kettle; a stainless steel sink; medical posters and a heavily annotated calendar on the walls. The young man crosses the room to a metal shelf unit and lifts down a white cardboard shoebox from the top shelf. 'He wanted to be sure you had this. Just a few personal things, I think. He was very concerned you should have them. He was afraid they might just be disposed of otherwise.'

'Thanks,' Richard says, taking the box. 'And thanks for all you're doing for him. I appreciate it.'

'Not at all,' the young man says. 'He's a nice old man, your uncle. It's been a privilege looking after him, a real learning experience, you could say. But then they all are, really.'

They shake hands and Richard opens the front door and steps out into the tiny front garden. The sky's turned from blue to pale grey in the short time since he arrived, the light's fading and there's the first autumnal chill of dusk in the air. There's no one about, no sound of cars moving or children playing; the houses, dark against the sky, have a deserted, threatening look. He shivers as he crosses the road. He unlocks his car, leans over and puts the shoebox on the front passenger seat, gets in and closes the door. If he was sensible, he'd set off for London right now, but he needs a drink before he gets going, needs that spell on his own he's been promising himself, and he turns the car and heads back down the hill towards the town centre. He passes the railway station, driving slowly, and fifty yards further on sees a pub sign, The Clayborne Arms. Someone pulls out from a parking-spot just ahead of him and he moves forward quickly to take it. He looks at the white shoebox with his name on it, then gathers it up and gets out of the car and walks the few yards back to the pub. He isn't thinking about the drive, or about getting home. No need to yet, he's earned this respite.

It's quiet in the pub. Two men standing at the bar who look like sales reps glance up and nod to him as he approaches. There's an old man in a shabby brown suit and flat cap sitting at a corner table with his half-pint of bitter. Richard orders a pint of Guinness and carries it with the shoebox to a table under a window. For a minute or so he sits with his eyes closed, waiting for the beer to settle. Then as he picks up his glass and drinks he feels the tension draining out of him. It's a sensation as much physical as mental: of muscles loosening, his head clearing, even his face relaxing. He drinks again, then puts down his glass and opens the shoebox.

There are photos inside, about forty or fifty of them, by the look of it. The first one he picks up, not much larger than a matchbox, shows a smiling, darkhaired boy of twelve or thirteen. He's wearing grey shorts and a white singlet and is holding a silver trophy in both hands. Richard turns the photo over and reads, 'Ronnie Wins The Mile Cup! –

July 1932.' The next photo shows his uncle as a soldier in beret and battledress, leaning against the side of a tank. 'Tobruk, 1941.' Then there's another picture from the war, Uncle Ronald and three other soldiers standing outside a church, arms round each others' shoulders, all of them grinning broadly and perhaps slightly drunkenly at the camera. 'Bari, 1943.' Richard looks at it for a while, then reaches into the box and takes out another photo. This one's in colour: Uncle Ronald with his wife Sheila, middle-aged, sitting on a garden bench in front of an ivy-covered stone wall. 'On holiday in Wells, August 1976'. Next there's a sepia-tinted studio portrait of his uncle as a small boy with his mother and father, all of them in their Sunday best and looking nervously solemn for the occasion; then a wedding-day photo, Ronald and Sheila cutting the cake; then Ronald and another man strolling along a sea-front. 'Ronnie and Bill Stephenson, Sidmouth, 1964.'

Richard puts the lid back on the box and picks up his glass. He isn't calm now, like he was before. They've come to an end, those few precious minutes of equanimity, leaving him with an edgy unsettled feeling. What does his uncle expect him to do with these pictures? Take them out and look at them once in a while? Keep them until he dies? Leave them to his wife or son when he dies?

He gets up and takes his empty glass back to the bar. Just one more pint, he's thinking, but as he hands the glass to the barman he changes his mind and asks for a double scotch. He pours half as much water again into the glass and takes it back to the table. He imagines himself living in this town and coming here every evening – the anonymous man who sits by himself, inscrutable, perfectly content in his isolation.

But too late for that, of course. The propaganda's seen to that – that and an unprecedented fear of being alone for ever which, as his thirtieth birthday came and went, was like an icy wind blowing through him. If he'd had the strength, or the foresight, to resist that fear and say, No, I stick by myself! his life would be different now, he'd be free of all these encumbrances. But what's the use in such thoughts? It's too late for them. It's too late for anything, really.

Sad, Alex will say, when he shows her the photos. 'Oh, it's so sad! And to think we just stopped inviting him!' Perhaps she'll cry a little, and if he shows no sign of sharing her sadness she'll tell him he's cold: a cold, unfeeling person, she'll call him. What she won't understand is that his uncle's life has been no more sad and meaningless than almost anyone else's. Seventy-something years adding up to nothing but tears and a collection of snapshots. Ronnie Wins The Mile Cup! Had it been the high spot of his life, aged thirteen?

He finishes his scotch, gets up and goes to the gents, then comes back through the bar and pushes the door open and leaves. He gets into his car and waits for a motorcycle to pass before pulling out. Fifteen minutes later the town's behind him and he's heading along the main road towards the motorway. Traffic's lighter than he'd expected, he might be home sooner than he'd thought.

A few miles on, he reaches out to switch on the radio and, glancing down at the passenger seat, realises he's forgotten the photos.

Shit!

He slows down, waving ahead the white BMW that's been hanging on his tail the last couple of miles. How much time will he lose, going back? Half an hour, he reckons, forty minutes maximum. He has to go back, though, for the photos. He can't not go back. There's a roundabout sign-posted ahead and he figures he'll turn when he gets to it. Half an hour should do it fine, he thinks, just as long as he can find a parking-space without too much trouble.

He should go back. That's the truth of it. He's doing the right thing. He tells himself, *You are doing the right thing!* and for a moment or two there's some surprising small pleasure in the thought. But then it vanishes and a feeling of the most profound disgust takes hold of him. It's a feeling almost blinding in its force, and inexplicable, and although he still has it in mind to turn, when he reaches the roundabout he doesn't turn but keeps going straight ahead. His breathing slows. He imagines someone finding the pictures and handing them in to the landlord who will keep them for a while in case someone claims them and then one day shrug and throw them out. *Well, all right,* he thinks. *Okay, then.* He turns the radio on, hums along with the anodyne music, taps his finger on the wheel as he drives towards the place where he lives.

Dancing

'You don't dance?' the young woman said. She paused,
giving N. an incredulous and it seemed to him scornful
look. 'Not at all?' she said. 'Not ever?'

'I'm afraid not,' N. said, meeting her gaze because there
was little choice but to meet it and striving for an unruffled
indifferent tone.

The woman stared at him for what seemed a long time,
still with the same look on her face, then turned and walked
back towards the crowded dance-floor where people were
standing around waiting for the music to start again. N.
stayed at the bar sipping his drink. He hadn't wanted to
come to this party and told himself that if he'd known that it
involved dancing he certainly wouldn't have come. But it
was his first Christmas with the company and he'd accepted
the invitation because it had been easier than declining it.
He didn't want people thinking he was strange in some
way, or thought himself too superior to everyone else to
share in the celebrations. Now he thought that if only he'd
been able to think clearly, instead of panicking as he had,

he would have accepted and then got out of attending by phoning in that morning and saying he was ill.

The party was in one of the function rooms of a large and depressingly characterless hotel, the sort of place, N. imagined, to be found in any large city. There were about eighty of them there. There'd been a sit-down three-course meal, utterly mediocre in N.'s opinion. Then there'd been three or four speeches by the directors, each of whom had tried to hit a humorous, democratic note. People had laughed when they thought it appropriate to laugh and had applauded dutifully as each speech came to an end. After the speeches, the tables had been cleared and pushed up against the walls, appallingly loud music had started playing and almost everyone had jumped up to dance as if everything that had gone before had been no more than a prologue to the real point of the evening. Apart from N., almost the only ones who hadn't taken to the dance-floor were those who were a good few years older than him, people who doubtless had danced in their younger days but lacked the energy for it now and were able to sit back and watch without anyone thinking that it was only an unhealthy inhibition that kept them from dancing. Twenty years from now N. might be able to claim the same right for himself, but not yet. He was thirty-six and wished he looked older than his age rather than younger. People made assumptions about you when you looked young, all the wrong assumptions in his case.

It mystified him how anyone could actually enjoy this sort of dancing, which involved nothing more than throwing oneself around the floor paying little or no attention to one's supposed partner, and it struck him as he watched how incredibly lacking in grace most people were when they danced. Here, for example, was a fat girl of perhaps twenty-two or –three, wearing a ridiculously tight, ridiculously short skirt, sweating as she performed a clumsy and to N.'s eyes painfully self-conscious imitation of the dancers she'd seen on television, or perhaps at venues such as this, while two feet away from her a slim young man who had shoulder-length jet-black hair and was wearing a close-fitting blue suit danced without even looking at her. All he looked at as he moved was his own body, his own gestures, as if he believed every movement wonderful. The poor girl was not by any definition his partner; she was there to show *him* off, that was all he wanted from her, and probably, N. thought, the more clumsy she was the better he liked it.

Once as he was looking on, N. caught sight of the woman who had asked him to dance. She and her partner were dancing close together to the sort of music usually described as 'smoochy'. N. saw her move closer still and whisper into her partner's ear. 'Talking about me, probably,' he thought and waited for the man to turn to look at him. Nothing happened, however, they continued dancing and N. thought, 'Well, of course, why should either of them care?'

No one else asked N. if he'd like to dance, and although one or two people spoke to him briefly when coming to the bar for drinks, for the most part he was alone. The entire experience was absurd and oppressive; he had no place in such a gathering and he couldn't understand why those responsible for organising it hadn't stopped and recon-sidered. People who liked to dance didn't need to wait for events such as the firm's annual party, they could go dancing every evening, if they wished. It would have been cheaper to organise a party in the office. It would have been cheaper, and as much to everyone's satisfaction, surely, to have dropped the idea of a party altogether and increased everybody's Christmas bonus by a small amount. But of course things weren't done that way. There had to be this emphasis that they were all in it together – a 'team' – this demonstration that the people at the top of the company were just like everyone else at heart, could let their hair down and be as familiar with the most junior members of staff as they were with each other. Which surely no one believed but which for these few hours each year they persuaded themselves they did believe so as not to diminish their enthusiasm for the evening. But what of those who, even though as hardworking as anyone else, had no desire to think of themselves as part of a team? The answer, of course, was that it was not compulsory to attend the Christmas party, but it was an answer that took no account of the degree of mental toughness required if one was swim to against the tide by declining. And if someone did choose not to attend, N. believed, then it would be noted that they were not team players, would be remembered when assessments were carried out and pay-rises and promotions considered.

Because he was alone, N. was drinking more quickly than usual. For a while he tried to force himself to slow down, but without anything else to focus on it was impossible. Then he decided that he didn't care anyway; there was nothing to do except drink and, far from befuddling him in any way, drinking seemed to have brought an extraordinary clarity to his thoughts. He was thinking things which previously he had only felt, without ever putting them into words. Nevertheless the time was passing dismayingly slowly. He watched the seconds ticking by on the electric clock behind the bar; then he resisted looking at the clock for what seemed an age, and when he did finally look at it again only seven minutes had gone by. He felt as though he had been here all his life and would be here for the rest of it. Once he looked over to where a small group of the other non-dancers were sitting; they were talking animatedly together, bursting into laughter now and then; their laughter was drowned by the relentless music but it was obvious to N. that they were enjoying the evening. He pictured himself crossing the floor to join them and, on arriving, being urged to pull up a chair: all perfectly possible, no reason at all why he shouldn't just pick up his glass and go, except that his nature prohibited him from doing it as surely as if he were not just standing at the bar but chained to it.

Ten o'clock came, then ten-thirty and at last eleven. N. wondered if the dancing would stop soon, giving people time to have one last drink, one brief period of general sociability, before gathering up their things and departing. But the music persisted, its merciless repetitive percussion even louder. More than ever he wondered at the sheer asininity of these people and was angered by the knowledge that even if they were to live a thousand years they would never see it for themselves. What had he done, to allow himself to be brought to this place? How had it happened, and when would he be released? The room could have been booked until the small hours, for all he knew.

He rose from his bar-stool, steadying himself with one hand on the bar, made his way along the edge of the room and then across the hotel foyer to the lavatory where he splashed cold water on his face and stood for several seconds looking at himself in the mirror. It struck him, as it always did when he confronted it like this, as a face that was different from other faces. Always the same pale, apprehensive look, the same weak chin and restless watchful eyes. It looked like the face of someone who expected at any moment to be dragged out of hiding and brought to public trial – not for any specific crime he could think of, but simply for being the person he was, for lacking those qualities which everyone else possess-ed and which indeed were indispensable if one was to consider oneself truly alive. The absence of those qualities – of the capacity for fun, of the preparedness to face such challenges as might present themselves, of the ability at the very least simply to feel at ease with others now and again – boiled down to the single bleak truth that he was afraid of living. And there was no remedy for this fear, the very best he could hope for was that he'd be able to avoid having to face it from time to time.

If he could only get out of here! But no sooner had the thought occurred to him than he realised that in fact he could. There was no need even to go back to the party before he escaped, no need for anything but to collect his coat from the cloakroom, leave the hotel by the main door and make his way home. Then on Monday he would explain to the others in his department that he'd been taken ill suddenly and had had no choice but to leave. They would believe him, or would pretend they did. It was all so per-fectly simple that N. couldn't understand why he hadn't thought of it before.

Five minutes later he had left the hotel and turned the corner on to a wider, busier street where he now stood waiting for a taxi. One came almost at once, and stopped

for him, and N. clambered into the back and gave the driver
his address. As the taxi moved off and gathered speed, he
leaned back closing his eyes and letting out a sigh of relief.
Nothing more ahead of him tonight, except his flat and
solitude; nothing more he wanted than that. Past closed
shops they moved, past pubs and cinemas whose windows
and fascias were darkened. N. wanted to tell the driver just
to keep on going, to leave the city and drive anywhere,
anywhere at all – to drive for ever, so that he could look out
of the window and watch the scene vanish as instantly as it
presented itself to him, now here, now gone. No one would
wonder who that person was in the speeding car, or where
he was going; challenges would cease to exist, obligations,
the whole tyrannical charade of his life. N. surrendered to
this vision, actually believing for a moment that it could be
made permanent, but now the taxi was turning into the street
where he lived, a street of large and rather ugly Victorian
houses, and with an effort he leant forward and told the
driver where to stop. His flat was on the top floor of the
house, a large loft-space which had been made into a bed-
sitting-room with an open-plan kitchen at one end and a
shower-room and lavatory off to one side. N. closed the
door behind him and sank into a chair. He was conscious of
being drunk now, though not in a way that made him feel
ready for sleep. Quite the reverse: a kind of restlessness
had taken hold of him, almost a feverish state: not happiness exactly, it was too insubstantial for that, but a kind of
ecstasy of relief such as an escaped prisoner might feel, so
intoxicated by his new-found freedom that it hasn't occurred
to him to wonder how long it might last or what he should
do with it.

N. closed his eyes. When he opened them again, he realised he'd been sleeping but didn't know for how long. He didn't feel so good any more. The heating had gone off and the room was cold. He was cold, to the very pit of his stomach. A certain mood had descended on him, as familiar as this room where he was sitting but none the easier for that. That there was no one here to keep him company was the very least of it; he was used to having no company but his own and often believed he preferred it since, whatever its penalties, at least solitude was safe. But what he was feeling now, and had felt periodically for years – when he got into bed and turned the lamp off, for example, or woke in the morning, or turned the corner into a street that was empty, or let himself into the flat after coming back from work – what he was feeling now was the loneliness not of someone alone in a room but of someone alone in the world. Truly he was convinced that there was no one out there, that if he were to go downstairs and open the door there would be nothing to see, no people, no houses or parked cars, no trees, fences, lamp-posts, traffic-lights, pavements – nothing but a landscape empty and everlasting as the desert or some vast tract of ice, where not a sign of life was to be seen.

N. clutched his knees. He rocked back and forth in his chair, his head lowered. He tried to calm his breathing, which was too fast, too loud. As always, he told himself it was ridiculous to feel as he did. He lived in a city of almost a million people, for God's sake, where often it seemed that the crowds, the noise, were scarcely to be borne. Had all these people disappeared? Could the city itself actually have vanished? He tried again to remember when he had first suffered this illusion; sometime in childhood, he felt. It must have begun in childhood, because it was the sort of fear you could well imagine seizing a child. But not an adult. Not someone thirty-six years old who'd found no way of dealing with that childish terror but to wait for it to end.

Without thinking N. got up and went to the kitchen and switched on his little battery-run radio. A song known to him was playing – it was Doris Day singing 'Secret Love', a romantic slow-tempo song that he remembered being popular twenty or thirty years ago.

Instead of returning to his chair, N. stayed close to the radio, listening. After a few seconds, as if of its own accord, his left leg lifted itself tentatively forward, bent at the knee, and when it returned to its place the other leg performed the same movement. The legs continued to alternate like that and – again without N.'s volition – his arms started moving, lifting themselves until his hands were as high as his shoulders, at which point they began describing languorous circles in the air. N. realised he was dancing – not that well perhaps, and certainly far too self-consciously, but surely no more badly than some he had seen (the fat girl at the party, for instance). It was a strange feeling, and while he was still wondering what to make of it the music faded out and a different number began, a fast, raucous number, featuring saxophones and drums and guitars and the single word 'boogie!' shouted at intervals. N.'s dancing changed. His self-consciousness miraculously disappeared and with it his awkwardness. He danced his way across the room to the wardrobe and jerked it open so as to see himself in the full-length mirror on the inside of the door. It astounded him how well he was dancing, his arms and particularly his legs moving in ways he wouldn't have thought possible, his hips swivelling as if he'd been a dancer for years. 'Boogie!' he shouted along with the band, not feeling absurd in the least.

When the number ended, he turned the radio off and sat down again. Presently, as though making an announcement to the people from work who had suddenly appeared before him, he said flatly: 'I dance alone.' The words had a self-possessed, unequivocal tone which pleased him. 'I dance alone,' he repeated and the woman took an involuntary step backwards, clapping her hand to her mouth in a childlike gesture. Her shoulders slumped and her face took on a bewildered, humiliated look. N. picked up his drink and watched her walk back unsteadily in her high heels to where her companions were waiting. Quite likely, he thought, it was these same companions who, sensing that he'd be embarrassed at being asked to dance, and looking forward to a few moments' amusement at his expense, had in fact dared her to ask him. Well, it had rebounded on them, and serve them all right. He smiled and those standing alongside him at the bar turned to him and smiled too, as if in admiration of the way he'd dealt with that foolish woman. He didn't move from his chair, just leaned back closing his eyes, content, not even thinking of moving.

Exits

What can I say about him, except that he lived here for a time and then died here? There's almost nothing to say. He was a stranger to us, from first day to last.

Of course we used to see or hear him coming in and out from time to time, and sometimes when I was out I would see him on one of the streets near our house. He was always polite on those occasions, wishing me *Buenas Dias* or *Buenas Tardes*, with a little bow of his head. Once he saw me from across the street and hurried over to carry home my shopping for me, a distance of a quarter-mile or so, which we walked together in a silence neither one of us could break.

When the rent was due, he would come down and knock on the door of our kitchen on the exact day and give us an envelope with the money in it. He would smile, handing us the money; *Gracias*, he would say, or *Muchas gracias*; then he would pause – hesitate – like someone on the very brink of saying something more. It seemed a long time, standing there waiting for him to speak. Even though he was probably close to fifty years old, he seemed more like a boy during those moments, a nervous teenage boy who feels he should be able to speak with the grown-ups on equal terms but can't find the words, or is afraid of saying something that will sound clumsy, or comical, and can only blush and stare at his shoes and eventually mumble something inaudible and turn away. That was the impression he gave, and often afterwards I found myself wishing I had asked him to come into the kitchen and have a cup of coffee with us, a little conversation perhaps, through which we might learn at least something of each other. But I never did ask him in. Perhaps after all he was just a very private person and didn't really want to say anything. But there are things you sense in people, and in him I seemed to sense nothing but loneliness and what I can only call fear. His face always wore the same strained, haunted look, even when he smiled, as if he were in the grip of forces he could neither control nor escape. But I ignored my feelings, mainly because I knew my husband would not have been pleased with me if I had asked him in. Probably it would have made no difference anyway, but who could put their hand on their heart and say they know that for sure?

*   *   *

We'd put a notice in our window, apartment for rent; he came and knocked on our door one evening and after I had led him upstairs and shown him the apartment, he said he would like to take it. He was not working, he said, but he had money and it would be no problem paying the rent. (All this took some time, as sometimes he stopped to consult a pocket dictionary he had with him, and now and again he forgot himself and spoke a few words in English, or tried to make himself understood by using a gesture in place of words.) I was glad to have found someone so quickly, the notice had been in the window for only three or four days, but when I went downstairs to tell my husband the news he wasn't as pleased as I'd hoped he would be. An American, he said, pronouncing the word as always as though he would choke on it. And not working. How could we trust him? How could we tell if we could trust him? How did we know he didn't have some bad reason for coming to our country which might make trouble for us too one day? American, he said again, but just at that moment the man appeared in the doorway and told us he was not an American. *No Americano*, he said, *Ingles* and took out his passport and showed it to us. England, he said. *Inglaterra.* Then he took some money from his wallet and held it out to us, saying he would pay two months' rent there and then, and my husband agreed. I know that there are many good reasons for hating the Americans, and that my husband is by no means alone in hating them; but of England we knew almost nothing and had no feelings one way or the other for its people. And we needed the money. My husband has an illness of the lungs and had been unable to work for more than two years at the time I'm speaking of. There is a pension, miserably small, and sometimes he does some work for others in the neighbourhood, shopkeepers or small businessmen, who want someone to prepare their accounts or fill in their tax forms. which in fact is what he is doing for someone today. But it has always been hard for us since he fell ill. That was why he borrowed from his brother to have a little kitchen made on the top floor and a bathroom for ourselves on the ground floor, because we could get more money for an apartment than for a room and whoever lived in it would not have to share our own kitchen and bathroom.

The next morning a taxi arrived and our lodger got out and unloaded his belongings. There were two suitcases, one large, one not quite so large, a cardboard box, and a typewriter in its case. It seemed not very much for a man his age, especially one who had told us he expected to be staying for some time in our country, and later that day my husband said it looked as though he had had to get away quickly from somewhere. Who knows, he said, we might have a man on the run living in our house, a criminal. I laughed, telling him he had too much imagination for his own good. You have been watching too much television, I told him, trying to make a joke of it, but still he sat there leaning forward with his hands clasped under his chin, frowning. Anyway, I said, we will have the money coming in, we can start paying your brother what we owe and when we've finished paying we'll have still more money. To which my husband answered: Yes, but never enough.

We sat in silence then, as we had done more and more often since he had to stop working. He saw his inability to provide for us as failure, as if it was his fault he'd fallen ill. I understood that, and I understood that the giving up of the top floor of our house to a stranger, forcing us to restrict our belongings and our lives to the ground floor, only increased that sense of failure. My husband was filled with a bitterness and self-loathing which, from all I saw, had turned into a loathing of life itself. And I couldn't blame him, to tell the truth. I'd seen how he struggled for breath sometimes, exhausted by some task he would have carried out easily before he fell ill; then afterwards he would lie back on the sofa fighting for breath while I wiped his forehead with a dampened cloth, and held his hand, and did whatever else I thought might comfort him. Little by little his breathing would slow and quieten and he would look at me with the face of a child whose suffering can't be explained, a dazed, terrified face. But when he saw the tears starting to my eyes, his face would harden and he'd remove his hand from mine. Don't fuss, he'd tell me. I'm all right. I'm fine, now. It's nothing. Don't make a fuss. He shut me out in this way and I didn't blame him for that either, for all that it hurt.

*   *   *

During the next few days our lodger was in and out of the house, going out quite early in the morning and returning with things he had bought for his apartment: food, pots and pans and crockery and so on. From the window one day I saw him get out of a taxi and carry a record-player into the house, and later, as my husband and I were eating our supper, the sound of music reached us from upstairs, classical music, with a choir singing. I didn't know what piece of music it was, or who had composed it; but not long afterwards when my cousin Carlos was visiting us, and the same music was playing, he told us it was the Mass in B Minor, by Bach. Wonderful, he said and leaned back in his chair and closed his eyes. You have a lodger with immaculate taste, he said, and I smiled at that, though my husband's face remained as stony as ever.

As well as the music there was also the sound of his typewriter, sometimes for three or four hours at a time. My husband would roll his eyes towards the ceiling, muttering that if we had to share our house with a stranger, then at least surely we could have found one who would leave us in peace. He complained so often that I lost patience with him eventually, telling him that our lodger had a life of his own, just as we had, and that we must allow him to live it. Besides, I said, if the sound of a record-player or a typewriter was the worst we had to put up with, we should count ourselves lucky. We might have taken on a lodger who liked to give parties in his apartment, or who played much louder music, that same sort of music, so-called, that you hear blaring from car radios or from the doorways of certain shops. My husband grunted in reply, and to change the subject I said that our lodger struck me as a very troubled person, very much alone in the world. No friends coming to see him, not even a letter, in all this time: surely he deserved his small pleasures, which after all were not as intrusive as my husband liked to say they were. My husband gave me a look of contempt. Troubled? he said. Who can pay his rent without even having to work for it? Who can go out and buy whatever he wants, live wherever he pleases? If that's what it is to be troubled, I would dearly love to be troubled.

I didn't answer at once. But then after a moment I said that perhaps he only noticed the noise so much because he was indoors almost the whole day, all through those hours when most men were out of the house and working. I will never forgive myself for those words, nor will I forget my husband's face as he heard them; it was like the face of someone dealt a blow almost too great to endure. I could hear his breathing and I saw him biting down on his lower lip and closing his eyes.

Dearest, I said, knowing that whatever words I might find they would not be enough. Dearest, I'm sorry. I didn't mean it. Truly I didn't. I moved towards him, hoping that an embrace would count for more than words. But when I laid my hand on his shoulder he stiffened so violently that I had to take it away. No, you're right, he said. Of course you're right. I should have seen it myself. I'm a fool, he said, for not having seen it myself.

*   *   *

Life went on like that. The music, the typewriter, his footsteps on the stairs or the ceiling, his monthly knock on our door to pay the rent. My husband didn't complain any more, or at least not out loud. He read his newspaper every day – read it from cover to cover, as though every word was important to him – and spent hour after hour lying on the sofa watching television. Often he fell asleep while watching and I would have to wake him to tell him supper was ready. He ate without appetite, saying hardly a word to me. I tried from time to time to have a conversation with him, but he replied in such an abrupt indifferent voice that it was impossible to go on.

Every night he went to bed before me and was asleep by the time I entered the bedroom. When I woke each morning, he'd already gone out to buy his newspaper and had come back and made coffee for himself. Engrossed, or pretending to be engrossed, in his paper, he gave me only the briefest glance when I came and sat down. Sometimes when I wished him good morning, he didn't even bother to reply.

Punishment, was what it was. I understood that, and I didn't blame him for it. Not a day went by when I didn't tell myself I should have bitten my tongue off rather than speak to him as I had. It was right that I should be punished – indeed it was hard to see how I could ever be punished enough. If only I could have put my arms around him and somehow made him see that I loved him, that there were still pleasures to be found in living, if only the modest pleasures that were most people's lot. I imagined the two of us weeping together and being cleansed by those shared tears so that our lives would be changed – would be made new again. But of course this never happened, nor can I believe that it ever will happen.

Sometimes as we sat there in silence and I heard our lodger moving about over our heads, or the music or the typewriter going, I pictured myself running upstairs and knocking on his door and asking if I could come in for a while. Just a few minutes' companionship, a few minutes' talk: I longed for talk – not even to talk about anything important necessarily, just the simple exchange of words, which it seemed was lost to me for ever.

Once, and this is something I have never confessed to a soul, I did go upstairs and enter his apartment. It was mid-afternoon, he was out somewhere for once and my husband was sleeping. I crept upstairs carrying my shoes and, hardly daring to breathe, I opened his door and went inside. It surprised me how absolutely clean and in order everything was. In the kitchen there were no unwashed dishes left out; the sink and draining-board were clean, and so was every-thing else, including even the floor and the window. Everything was spotless, as though the apartment had been prepared for someone who had not yet arrived. In the main room, where he both lived and slept, the bed was made and the rug and the cushions had been placed on it to turn it into a sofa. On the small table close to the sofa were his typewriter and a jar filled with pencils and a stack of papers neatly arranged. Nothing out of place, not so much as a speck of dust anywhere. For a moment I thought how pleased my husband would be, if I were to tell him what a conscientious lodger we had. But of course I couldn't tell him, and even if I could have he wouldn't have been pleased because he'd come to a point where he didn't want anything to please him.

I sat down at the table, stared at the typewriter a while and ran my fingers over the keys. It must be something terribly important, I thought, to keep him typing away so many hours; and suddenly I felt that if I could just read and understand what he'd written, then something would be shown to me, something I should have seen for myself but had failed to see, which would make an enormous difference to my life. You'll probably think I was stupid to get such an idea, and I'd have to agree. But there it was anyway, and at the time it didn't seem stupid. I looked at that stack of paper again, and although it made me feel more of an intruder than ever, I picked up the top sheet and tried to read it. Naturally it was in English and I couldn't understand more than two or three words; there was no knowing what he was writing that was of such importance.

When I got up again, I noticed a framed photograph on the window-ledge: two small boys side by side on a beach somewhere, both wearing shorts and T-shirts, both standing with folded arms and staring with tired, sullen faces at the camera. His sons, I supposed; I couldn't think who else they might be. I wondered how old the photograph was. I wondered where his sons were now, and his wife; if they were all living together somewhere in England, or if the sons had grown up by now and were living away from their mother. I wondered what had happened in that family, to take him so far from them. It made me shiver, that picture, even though the window was closed and the room hot and airless. I put the picture back in its place and left the apartment, picking up my shoes outside the door and creeping back downstairs. I don't think I can tell you what I was feeling. At first I thought it was just guilt at having spied on him, but later I realised it was more than that. I don't think I've ever felt so lonely in my life. Or more afraid, for that matter, though when I asked myself, Afraid of what? there was no answer.

*   *   *

Some time later we went to stay with my sister for a while, as we had almost every summer for years. She and her husband and their two boys live near a town just a short bus-ride from the sea, about four hours by train from here. I'd always enjoyed staying with them, but this time our visit was almost spoilt before it had begun when my husband told me he didn't really feel like going. He said, You can go on your own if you like, though he must have known I wouldn't dream of leaving him by himself. I tried to persuade him it might be good for him being by the sea for a time, especially now that it was so hot and humid in the city. A change of scene might do you good, I said, and he looked at me with an expression of pity on his face, as though wondering how I could be stupid enough to believe that something as insignificant as staying somewhere else for a while could make any difference. I'm fine as I am, he said, I don't need to go anywhere else. But he did agree, eventually; agreed for my sake, I believed, though later I thought no, that wasn't true, he was agreeing so as not to give me anything to hold against him which might cause me to forget what he held against me.

Every weekday while we were there my brother-in-law drove off to work in the morning, leaving us to spend the day as we chose. All of us, and especially the boys, wanted to go to the beach. Not my husband, though. You go on, he'd say, I think I'll just stay here and rest, if you don't mind. He was sitting at the breakfast table drinking a second or third cup of coffee and reading the newspaper, seemingly oblivious to his surroundings, while my sister and I washed the dishes and prepared some food to take to the beach, and the boys loitered outside with their football and their towels and swimming-trunks. I couldn't help thinking of those summers before his illness, when he'd swum with the boys, had even helped teach them to swim, and had been, or had seemed to be, as relaxed and good-humoured as the rest of us. But even after he'd fallen ill, he'd never been as silent and indifferent to us all as he was this time. More than once I caught myself thinking how much better we'd all feel if he'd stuck to his original decision and stayed at home; but always this thought was followed by the memory of how I'd spoken to him that day and I was left once again with the feeling that it wasn't him who was to be blamed for his behaviour, but me.

One day towards the end of our stay, when the boys had gone off to play at some other children's house, my sister and I went into town together. She made some lunch to take with us and when she'd finished her shopping we sat in a shady spot by the river to eat it. We talked about the boys, about her husband's job (which was wearing him out, she said), about a film she'd seen not long ago; then after a lull in the conversation, she asked about my husband. He seems – not himself, somehow, she said and gave me such a sad, troubled look that I could have burst into tears. It was beautiful, there by the river. Several rowing-boats were out, a motor-launch chugged by, its flag fluttering in the breeze off the water, and not far from where we were sitting some boys were jumping into the river shouting boisterously to each other. High up on the opposite bank, where many of the town's wealthier people lived, the trees and the elegant white houses among them looked more like a painting than real life – a painting you'd like to step into and live in, because everything in it looked so permanent and calm, beyond the reach of any kind of disturbance. I suppose it was due to the peace and unfamiliarity of the scene, but I couldn't help thinking as we sat there how easily life could be so much less burdensome than it was. Just a change of heart on someone's part, a softening of the heart, a refusal to give into those forces which achieve nothing but to push other people away and make one's own life a misery – how hard could that be? At the same time, though, I knew that life could never be any different. Even the people living in those beautiful houses high above us, for all their money, were probably no more at peace with themselves than anyone else.

It's as if he's locked the door on himself, my sister said. But why? There was that same concern in her voice, and in her face too, but I recalled at that moment how I'd seen her looking at my husband only two or three days ago, when she was washing the dishes and he was sitting at the table reading the newspaper, having yet again declined our invitation to come with us to the beach. It was the very briefest of looks, vanished almost as soon as it had appeared, but unforgettable: her mouth turned down, a look of scorn in her eyes, as if she were contemplating someone not even worth her pity. Remembering that look, I felt obliged to defend my husband, to make her see how hard life was for him. To have fallen ill so young, to be worried about money all the time, to have seen half his house taken from him, to feel, above all, that there was nothing in life left for him but to depend on others while contributing almost nothing himself – who could blame him, in the face of all that, for feeling as he did? Then, though it wasn't something I'd been planning to say, I told her of that terrible thing I'd said to him and of the awful look on his face after I'd said it. You mustn't pass judgement on him, I said. It's been hard for him. He doesn't deserve to be judged.

Maria, my sister said, and she reached out and placed her hand on mine. I don't judge him. It's for God, if he exists, to pass judgement. But what about you? You're passing judgement on yourself, aren't you? Condemning yourself, because once, and just for a moment, you lost control and said something not very nice. That isn't cruel, Maria. It's human. Certainly it's a lot less cruel than just shutting somebody out for months on end.

I could feel her eyes on me. I felt as though she was willing me to look back at her and tell her yes, she was right. But I couldn't look back at her. I wanted the conversation to end, more than anything else. The doubts, the

questions: they were too much for me, they made me feel
like a child, made me long to be a child again, living in a
world where such problems simply didn't exist.

My sister gathered up the food we hadn't eaten and
dropped it into a plastic bag. She tied the bag and got up
and put it into a litter-bin under the trees. He has his life,
she said, sitting down again. He has you. Doesn't that mean
anything to him? D'you think he can't see how much he's
hurting you, by cutting you off as he does? Does he have to
wipe out everything you've done for him – and are still
doing – to make you pay for just one thoughtless remark?

He has to choose, she said. But I was hardly listening by
then, and I didn't give the words any thought. We left the
river and talked about other, easier matters as we walked
home. It was a relief, just to be walking and talking like that.
I felt as though I'd been snatched from danger at the last
moment and brought back to safety.

*   *   *

Then we came home again, and then we found him.

It was the smell we noticed, when we opened the door.
The smell of something rotten in the house; not that strong,
there in the hall, but strong enough that it was impossible
not to notice it. At first we thought we must have left out
some food which had gone bad. Then when we couldn't
find anything we wondered if some small animal had found
its way into the house and died while we were away. We
searched everywhere, in cupboards, behind the furniture,
underneath the rugs, under a loose floorboard in the kitchen and another in the bedroom, but we didn't find any
animal.

My husband gestured up at the ceiling. It must be his place, he said and we both stood still in the hall, listening for any sound of him moving about up there, but hearing nothing.

I had a premonition then – it was almost as though I *knew* – but I didn't let myself dwell on it. Stupid imaginings, I told myself. Don't be stupid! But I was trembling as I began climbing the stairs and, as I climbed, the smell grew worse. I had to take out my handkerchief and hold it pressed over my nose and mouth to keep out the smell.

I stopped on the stairs and looked back at my husband, who was still standing in the hall. I think we have to go in there, I said, and told him that if he was to come too he should find something to cover his face. My husband hesitated a few seconds, staying where he was. Then he took his scarf from its peg and tied it over the lower half of his face and came to join me.

Be careful, I said, as he came up towards me. My heart was pounding. Be careful, dear.

The door was open when we reached the top of the stairs. What we saw when we went inside is impossible to describe. So is the smell, which didn't diminish even after we'd thrown both windows open.

Our lodger, fully dressed, was lying sprawled on the sofa. His face was something I won't even try to describe. I can't believe that it would serve any purpose, or that any normal person would want me to describe it. All I will say is that I thank God we didn't come home any later than we did.

My husband looked at our lodger's body and swore softly and steadily at it, using every obscenity I've ever heard. He went to the window, tore the scarf from his face, and leaned out and vomited down into the garden. I can't stay, he said. Not with that – that *thing*. He almost ran to the door. I'm going to telephone the police, he said, and I heard him clattering downstairs, moving as fast by the sound of it as when he still had his health.

There was paper everywhere. Fragments of paper, scattered all over the floor, and when I picked one of them up I saw the typed words of English on it and realised that all these fragments were what was left of those pages I'd last seen arranged so neatly on the table, next to his typewriter and the jar with the pencils in it.

I saw the records he'd played so often: fragments, too. Jagged, shiny black fragments, their edges poking out sharply from amid all that paper.

I saw an empty bottle next to the sofa. Whisky. I saw an empty bottle of pills nearby, and I wondered if he'd got drunk on the whisky then taken more pills than he'd intended and killed himself by accident.

I wished then that I could have stayed with him until the police arrived. It seemed wrong that he should be left all alone until they came; wrong that he had died all alone, with no one to turn to. It seemed nothing less than my duty to stay with him and wait; but I couldn't stay, because I knew I'd be sick and perhaps even pass out if I did.

As I turned to leave, I saw an envelope on the table with my husband's name and mine written on it. I took it downstairs with me and showed it to my husband, who looked at it and shrugged faintly, as if to say, What's it to me? The police are coming, he said, they're bringing an ambulance with them. I sat down by the window. Then I opened the envelope and found myself looking at more money than I'd ever seen at one time. I started to count it but stopped after a while, when it reached a total almost as large as would come to us in a year.

Look, I said, holding the money out to my husband. A look of surprise crossed his face then almost at once disappeared. How generous, he said bitterly. His face was white, his voice shaking. How nice of him, to pay so handsomely for having filled our house with his stink. Looking back, it's hard to believe he could have spoken like that at such a time. But then everything was hard to believe. I felt I was caught in a nightmare, to tell the truth, so the words didn't surprise me.

There was the sound of a car pulling up and my husband got up and went out into the hall. When I went to put the money back in the envelope I saw that there was a sheet of paper still in there and I took it out and unfolded it.

Perdone me, he had written. And lower on the page, what could only have been the same in English: Forgive me.

Nothing after that. Not even his name.

*   *   *

The apartment was empty for some time following our lodger's death – which of course I know from that note he left us was certainly no accident. The police asked their questions that day, searched the place briefly and took some of his things away with them – his passport and some other papers, the empty bottle of pills, I can't remember what else. The ambulancemen wrapped the body in some kind of transparent material, then zipped it up in a long canvas bag. They lifted it on to a stretcher and carried it downstairs and loaded it into the ambulance. Before leaving, they told my husband and me that the door to the apartment was sealed and that we must on no account try to go in there. Tomorrow, they said, men would come to fumigate the apartment and would take away everything in it to be burned.

You must stay somewhere else, one of them said. Have you any family nearby? Friends? My husband told them his brother and sister-in-law lived not far away and we would stay with them, if we could. Or we'll stay in a hotel, he said. A cheap hotel, if such a thing still exists.

After the ambulance had driven off, we went out into our little garden and sat there. I'd made some coffee and my husband had brought a bottle of rum from the cupboard. He poured some into his coffee and a little of his colour came back after he'd drunk it.

Bastard, he said. He poured himself another rum and coffee. Thinks everything's all right if you just hand over some money. Bastard. It seemed an unfair remark to me; but seeing the rage in his eyes, and hearing it in his voice, I didn't dare say so. After a while he got up and went into the house to telephone his brother and it was arranged that we'd stay with them for as long as was necessary. We moved into their house that same evening, taking as few things with us as we could.

*   *   *

We have a new lodger now, a polite unobtrusive young man who goes to work every morning and spends his evenings studying for his business diploma. Every Friday he takes the bus to the town where his parents live, about eighty miles south of here, and doesn't return until late on Sunday.

Things haven't much changed in the house. We used some of the money we'd been given to redecorate and refurnish the rooms upstairs, and my husband paid off a portion of our debt to his brother. I went to the main police-station and asked if it would be possible to pay for a proper funeral for our lodger, but I was too late. The body had already been cremated, and with the very minimum delay. I would surely understand why, they said, and I did, of course, but that didn't make me feel any less sad.

My husband talks to me a little more often perhaps, but with no warmth in his voice, none of the tenderness it held so long ago. I can't believe I'll ever know that tenderness again.

Once – it was just a few days ago – he came into the kitchen and found me there weeping. What's the matter? he asked roughly. What are you crying for?

I can't help it, I said. I can't stop thinking of that poor man. I can't stop thinking there might have been something we could have done. I was standing with my back to my husband and he came and stepped in front of me and took told of me by the shoulders. He didn't want any help, he said, in a harsh, contemptuous voice. Didn't want any and didn't deserve any.

I stared at him. What d'you mean, didn't want any? How can you say that?

He hadn't the right to kill himself. Look at what he had. Money. No need to work. He could have gone anywhere to live, could have gone back to England, if he'd wanted. Look at what he had, he repeated, his voice shaking. Look at what we have. What gives *him* the right?

Again I didn't dare argue with him. I blew my nose and

wiped my eyes and tried to compose myself. Thank the Lord, I was thinking, that he hadn't found me all the other times I'd suddenly burst into tears.

It's what he wanted, my husband said. And look what he did to *us* by doing it. D'you think he cared? D'you think he thought of us for so much as a moment?

Anyway, he said, he wanted to die and he died. It's what you'd call a happy ending, isn't it?

Those were his last words on the subject. Nothing will change how he thinks, or lessen the anger he's feeling. It seems like something personal somehow, almost as if he believed our lodger had taken his life for no other reason but to spite him.

He has to choose, my sister said, that day when we sat by the river. And I brushed the words away because I was angry with her for talking about my husband as she had. But now I wonder if there's any such thing as choice and, if there is, whether it's something that exists only for the braver and more fortunate beings in this world. Could that man really have chosen to die? Do I choose to live? Does my husband live as he does because it's the life he's chosen? It's what he wanted, my husband said, but it's occurred to me since then that if he really believes that, then perhaps he should believe it equally of himself. It's a question I could never ask him, but I'd dearly like to know how he'd answer if I did.

I am here, is all I know. Life goes on, and I try to cope with it one day at a time, as best I can. Sometimes, it's true, I feel a fatigue pressing down on me that feels close to the desire for death. It frightens me when that happens, but then I think of my husband again and realise that no matter how I feel, it's my task to look after him, that that's what I was put on earth for, if only because that's where my life has brought me. They confuse me, all these thoughts. They should be left to people more sophisticated and knowledgeable than I, who could make more sense of them, or at least not feel as though they're drowning in them, as I do. I am here, and I can wash and mend my husband's clothes, can shop and cook and keep the house clean and tidy for him, even if that's all I can do. But it counts for something, doesn't it? Or should do. Or so, when there's nothing to keep me occupied for a time and I'm driven to consider my life, I try to believe.

Evening

Both in their seventies now, brother and sister sit in high-back armchairs each side of a fireplace where a tall willow-pattern vase filled with dried flowers is standing. The two standard lamps are switched on, the dark-red velvet curtains are closed; there is the sound of rain falling outside; a sound so unvarying that it's more like an absence of sound. The woman sits with one hand resting on an open magazine in her lap, her eyes gazing down at a carpet of no distinguishable colour or pattern. Occasionally her eyes close for a time, then open with a look of surprise, bewilderment, as on the face of someone roused too abruptly from sleep. The man has a glass and a half-full bottle of red wine on the table beside him; also an octagonal glass ashtray with several cigarette-ends and spent matches in it. Both these people are tall and thin, 'gaunt,' it could be said, dressed in clothes of dark, sombre colours, grey and brown and dark-blue. The room is crowded with dark heavy furniture: the lamps, a glass-fronted mahogany cabinet filled with china, old-style sofa and chairs covered in a dull bottle-green fabric, a ceiling-high antique dresser with rows of pewter plates and dishes on it, a television set in an oak cabinet. On the mantel-piece, each side of the loudly ticking clock, are several framed monochrome photos: a small boy and girl standing at the edge of a lake, a wedding couple posing outside a church, an elderly woman sitting in a garden, a man in army uniform. As the clock on the mantelpiece strikes ten, the man rises from his chair with an air of purpose, moves swiftly to the television and turns it on. The woman looks up and closes her magazine. Both sit leaning forward slightly, eyes fixed on the screen, waiting.